# SPARK

By

Caridad Svich

*Santa Catalina Editions*

*An imprint of NoPassport Press*

*Spark* book copyright 2016 by Caridad Svich

*Spark* play copyright 2012, revised 2014 by Caridad Svich

Santa Catalina Editions/NoPassport imprint; www.nopassport.org

ISBN: 978-1-329-99681-6

**The Land of *Spark***

The flames of passion that stir the desire toward moral accountability in society – toward, for example, the indictment for war criminals that live quite comfortably among us fellow citizens with no shame attached to their names – seem to flicker in burning embers, as the 2012 election year faded away. The talk all summer prior to the election on the media-waves was centred on and about the "economy," yet rarely focused on the sixth of the US that is unemployed and/or living below the poverty level. Somehow, the "inconvenience" of poverty – its strange stigma – couldn't compete for attention with the perceived glamour of the race to the White House. Yet, poverty, in the richest country in the world, where outsized, heaping plates of food are served daily at restaurants and diners across the US, is very much with us. In plain view. And with it, also, the stories of over two million Americans who have fought in the 2nd Iraq and  Afghanistan wars since 2001, and the families of these Americans who have had to cope with trauma and its aftermath.

No mention was made at the 2012 Republican National Convention of the over two million Americans who have served in these two long-standing wars. Eric Fehrnstrom, Romney's advisor, was so bold as to defend on CNN on 2 September 2012, the omission of the wars at the RNC and in Romney's speech, especially the 11-year engagement in Afghanistan, due to the fact that to talk of war and especially these wars, was "unpopular."

While President Obama spoke at Fort Bliss immediately on the heels of the RNC to demonstrate his acknowledgment of our currently deployed service men and women, and veterans, and a military mom addressed the audience as introduction to First Lady Michelle Obama's speech on the first day of the DNC, both wars have taken on a rather theoretical presence in US culture as a whole. While 2008's "The Hurt Locker" won the Academy Award, it was by no means a box office wonder, and 2012's "Zero Dark Thirty" (both films directed by Kathryn Bigelow), despite its many achievements as a piece of filmmaking has been dogged by questions about the accuracy through which it portrays US government's use of torture. And although countless films, TV programs, books and other creative forms of expression have addressed and continue to address the lingering effects of these two wars on our society and culture, somehow they seem to have become phantoms of themselves in the US' collective communal discourse. Due to unpopularity? Is it more comfortable to talk about who will be on TV's next "Dancing with the Stars"? Or is there something else that has generated self-censorship in our society? Is it, as Rachel Maddow has called it in her 2012 book of the same name, a kind of "drift?"

These thoughts stirred on a humid night in New York City, where the occasional siren broke the otherwise pall of seeming quiet, as I worked on *Spark*, which centers on a returning female soldier from our recent wars, and her coming home to a family of little means, a family of sisters, living in a poverty-stricken region of the Carolinas. In November 2012, right in the thick of what was, by all seeming accounts, a tough Presidential election, *Spark* sustained 32 readings through a NoPassport theatre alliance scheme at diverse venues across the US and abroad, including ones in New York City, Omaha, Boston, Portland, Chicago, Salt Lake City, Nagodoches, and even western Australia. With actor-producer Gloria Mann (spearheading a special reading/event at the Cherry Lane Theatre in New York City on November 11, 2012), line producer Lanie Zipoy, dramaturg Zac Kline, assistant dramaturg Erin Kaplan holding the ropes to this life-raft of a play, we engaged with a wide range of artists as well as communities of many shapes and sizes: of little, middling and more than middling economic means, with students, veterans, arts practitioners and families in the hope that this little story of faith and healing, hunger, forgiveness, trauma and reconciliation could be part of a larger conversation, one that moved past the reading room floor, and into the coffeehouse and street, about how living with war , even at home, when it is miles and miles away, is not a theoretical enterprise, but one that has real costs on a physical and emotional level, and one that – no news here, but history bears repeating – demands we take into account the reasons behind why these wars are fought and how, when they are fought, and that the damage that is effected is not only "over there," but on the home-front as well. However much the clarion calls of the respective 2012 political campaigns stressed the need to go forward as a nation without too long of a backward glance, strategic omission will not make the damage go away. It will only make the process of healing much more complex than it already is proving to be. *Spark* is the third play in this quartet of plays that focus on individuals who live in the burning holes of our torn fabric. All of the plays in this have been written out of an increasing sense of outrage – over the continued, seemingly convenient and remarkable (if you think about the fact that we live in the era of "advanced" communication) invisibility of stories on many of our arts platforms of those who live amongst us, with us, next to us, and who have perhaps the most to teach us, by dint of their experience, lives, and circumstances, about who we are, in the here and now, who we have been, and who we can be as a culture.

I don't mean to say that only those who have suffered a great loss, lost their livelihood, have been beset by human-made and natural disaster, or who have experienced and witnessed in their own flesh and blood the devastating nature of war itself, are the only figures that are worthy of recording in our books. Such a claim would be rash, unforgiving and freakily ennobling of loss, poverty and trauma as the only viable literary, cinematic and/or dramatic subjects that can merit and effect and/or contribute to a measure of cultural reparation. Moreover, while the impetus for this quartet has come from a need to draw attention to something in our culture and desire for it to have a hearing (one of a writer's essential duties, after all), at day's end, I do not pretend to be a journalist, and to do a journalist's or documentarian's job, but rather to come at and through my outrage from a poet's position: seeking the truths in and between the lines and their breaks, through acts of speech and gesture, and ultimately through a spiritual engagement with fictional characters drawn in flesh and blood.

In *Spark,* a young woman named Lexie Glimord comes home from her military service to a family of sisters eking out a living in a town where the divide between the haves and have-littles has grown increasingly more egregious over the years. The bonds among the three sisters in this play are fraught with tensions unresolved, a history of living in poverty, and a legacy of old-timey songs and incandescent spirituality handed down by their long-dead mother. The sparks of love and life flicker here, along with those of confusion and shame, as the Glimord sisters try to move on, whilst embracing their past and what they all have respectively gone through.

Theatre is often about what hurts – in society, in us as human beings, etc. It is a forum of public, live (even if it incorporates elements that are pre-recorded) engagement with wounding. Genet said it way back when. Euripides said it. And so on. Hurt doesn't go away.

Societies can heal, to an extent, perhaps even momentarily, perhaps even for a decade or two, at least on the surface, but there's also the "tear in the fabric," as Mark Ravenhill once said in his essay of the same name (2004) – and that tear is what theatre-makers are after. Not because the tear is sexy or popular or on trend, or even, shall we say cynically, remotely good fodder for a grant application. No. The tear (as in tears that sting your eyes, as in the hole that burns through a piece of cloth) is what gives the artist pause, and allows a space for open-ness that can thereafter allow for the space of creation, and down the pike create the space of invitation for the public to walk in and be able to, indeed, witness, participate and sit with/walk with/stand with (whatever the physical situation of the live experience may be) the unfinished work of spiritual engagement.

When a community has stopped functioning, however, the job and daily practice of art-making becomes doubly difficult because the artist is not only dealing with the recognition of the tear in the fabric – and that spark of recognition is key – and how to respond to the recognition with imagination, skill, talent, craft and discipline, but also with the almost insoluble fact that the work itself is not, cannot do the job, as it would in an operative situation. For example, if you are making theatre in a conflict zone, where, say, there are bullets being fired, then your choices have to be different, because the job of healing cannot be done in the same manner as if one were in a what for all intents and purposes in a controlled and "safe" environment.

If you live in an community that is merely functioning somehow, and you have come to at least recognize that fact, then what kind of work do you choose to make, and why? Do you make work that reinforces the nature of the community? Or do you go about an alternate method?

Theatre is a call to action. An action of the spirit. It takes all manner of ambition to assume that a piece of theatre in and of itself can "do" anything. A theatre piece, after all, is merely a score, an offering for a potential performance. It exists purely in ephemera: as mere signs on a page (if you're working with text). It is, by nature, "useless," (in regard to the workings of capital). And it takes a strong measure of grand folly to dedicate your life to a useless endeavor. And yet, I would argue, as have so many in history's long stream, that the uselessness and simultaneous usefulness of theatre-making, and one's dedication to its purpose, can sustain a life and the lives of others, if not monetarily, then at least through the very engagement and acknowledgment of the tears that we need shed and repair in our communities.

Caridad Svich

## Script History:

*Spark* was commissioned independently by Elaine Avila, Daniel Banks, Raymond Dooley, Amparo Garcia-Crow, Amy Gonzalez, Peter Lichtenfels, Charlotte Meehan, Christi Moore, Flor De Liz Perez, Marisel Polanco, Teresa Perez-Frangie, Otis Ramsey-Zoe, Claudio Raygoza, J.T.Rogers, Meghan Wolf and Tamilla Woodard.

It is inspired by the author's short monologue "Wonder" commissioned by CenterStage in Baltimore for the 2012 My America project, where it was filmed by Hal Hartley for Possible Films and performed by Flor De Liz Perez.

It was developed, in part, at the Lark Play Development Center and New Dramatists in New York City.

The play sustained 32 readings as part of a NoPassport theatre alliance reading scheme between October 22nd and November 30th, 2012 at venues across the US, including Cherry Lane Theatre in New York City (produced by TECL), Tricklock Theatre in Albuquerque; Stages Repertory in Houston; Profile Theatre in Portland; Bump in the Road Theatre in Baltimore; Trap Door Theatre in Chicago; and the Playwrights Center in Minneapolis, MN, and abroad in Seoul, Korea; Merredin, Western Australia; and London, UK. The line producer for the NoPassport scheme was Lanie Zipoy. The lead dramaturg was Zac Kline. For blog archive and more, visit http://www.nopassport.org/spark

This script received the 2013 National Latino Playwriting Award (sponsored by Arizona Theatre Company). It also received the 2013 Todd McNerney Playwriting Award (sponsored by the College of Charleston School of the Arts) with a reading at the Piccolo Spoleto Festival in Charleston, South Carolina.

SPARK received its premiere at Theater Alliance at Anacostia Playhouse in Washington D.C. in September 2014 under Colin Stanley Hovde's direction.

Revised version of the script received production at PYGmalion Productions in Salt Lake City, Utah in October 2014 under Fran Pruyn's direction.

*Spark*: Full-length in two acts. Cast: 3 women (1 late teens, 1 mid 20s, 1 30s), 2 men (1 30s, 1 late 40s). One central but slightly flexible location. Inclusive casting preferred. Running time: approx. 110 minutes.

Synopsis:

*Spark* is a play about three sisters living in the US caught in the mess of a recent war's aftermath. It is about what happens when soldiers come home, when women of little economic means must find a way to make do and carry on, and the strength, ultimately, of family. A contemporary US story of faith, love, war, trauma, and a bit of healing.

Characters:

EVELYN JANE GLIMORD, 31, older sister, the head of the house, proud, hard-working, frayed, dutiful; she feels as if the fabric of her world may tear at any second.

ALIYAH "ALI" MARGARET GLIMORD, 18, younger sister by 13 years, a boxer, rebellious, confused, acting out, with a sweet streak.

ALEXANDRA "LEXIE" RAY GLIMORD, 23, middle sister by 8 years, soldier, volatile, possesses a desire to move past her current station in life but is not sure how. Been away from home, in military service, for five years. At a crossroads.

HECTOR JOHNSON, 33, neighbor, friend of Evelyn's, honest, sensual, hard-working man with a sly sense of humor, possesses an essentially good-natured disposition.

VAUGHN, 48, a former soldier, a spectre.

## Time & Place:

The present, in a small town in North Carolina, situated somewhere along Interstate 40, also known as the "Tobacco Road."

## Settings:

Part One is set in the field behind the Glimord house. Part Two is set on the porch of the Glimord house, on a small hill near a river, where the town cemetery sits, and once again, in the field behind the house.

## Notes:

Melodies to the short, original songs in the text may be obtained by contacting the author or the lyrics may be re-set by another composer. Although the play on the surface has a realistic surface, it is encouraged that, in production, the setting have a strong element of abstraction, and/or something that is evocative of a ritualized and/or ceremonial playing space. It is preferred if the play is performed without an interval.

This play is the third in an "American quartet" of plays that includes the author's *GUAPA, The Way of Water,* and *Hide Sky.*

# Part One

## Scene One

*EXT. Early evening. In the foreground, a modest table, flanked by a handful of chairs, sits in the wild, slightly overgrown field behind the Glimord house. An equally modest pastel-colored plastic tablecloth adorns the table. A string of multi-colored lit paper lanterns is hung between the trees framing the table at a slightly oblique angle. (Note: the trees may be unseen; the string of lanterns could appear as if they were suspended in the air). In the b/g perhaps are seen the outlines of a simple house.*

*EVELYN walks in, singing an improvised tune, which sounds somewhat like a hymn. [Note: The song could be "Where I Go," which she sings later in the play.] She has a candle in one hand, encased perhaps in a jar, and a basket filled with party decorations in the other. She sets the basket down, and sets the candle on the table. Continuing her hymn, she pulls a box of matches from her pocket, slips open the box, pulls out a match and tries to light the candle. She fails.*

*ALIYAH (ALI) walks in, from the house. She carries a six-pack of beer. She watches. EVELYN does not see her.*

*Evelyn tries to light match again. She fails.*

EVELYN *(to herself)*: Can't see nothin'.

ALI: Don't know what you're doin' all this for.

*Ali sets six-pack down, to one side.*

EVELYN: Doin' ALL THIS 'cuz Lexie comin' back home after bein' in that war all that time. Want me to make like it's every day?

ALI: Let me.

EVELYN: Got it.

ALI: Evelyn.

EVELYN: Said I-!

*Evelyn tries to light match again. She succeeds. She lights the candle and sets it in the center of the table.*

EVELYN *(CONT, to herself)*: There. Don't that look nice?

*At some point during the following, Evelyn will pull items from the basket and decorate the table with paper napkins, party favors, miscellaneous things…*

ALI: Ain't.

EVELYN: What?

ALI: In a war.

EVELYN: Huh?

ALI: Lexie. She's in a "conflict."

EVELYN: Call it what they like. It's war. … What the hell is this six-pack doin' [here]?

ALI: Lexie likes beer.

EVELYN: Lexie likes a lot of things. But this is a special day. Go on. Get somethin' nice.

ALI: Evelyn…

EVELYN: Woman come back from drinkin' God-knows-what over there, we are not puttin' beer on the table, much less this beer. Down in the cellar. There's a nice bottle of cider. Bring that out.

ALI: Cider?

EVELYN: In the icebox down there. You'll see it.

ALI: When'd you-?

EVELYN: I buy things.

ALI: What you doin' goin' round buyin'-?

EVELYN: It was on special, okay?

ALI: That's our savin' up money…

EVELYN: Don't you be tellin' me what to do, girl. I don't see you workin'.

ALI: I'm lookin' for-

EVELYN: Yeah. But right now, I'm the one who's doin'…

ALI: Piddley jobs…

EVELYN: Piddley, but it's somethin'. Now, go on. Get the cider.

ALI: That candle smells.

EVELYN: And take this godawful beer out of here.

*ALI grabs six-pack and walks away, back toward the house.*

EVELYN (CONT, *calling out*): And bring the rhubarb pie while you're at it.

ALI: It's coolin.'

EVELYN: Done coolin' by now. … Knives and forks, Ali.

ALI: Yeah.

*ALI walks toward the house until she is gone from view.*

*A moment.*

EVELYN *(to herself)*: Don't know what she's talkin' about the candle "smells."

*She hovers over the candle for a bit. She likes the way it smells. From another part of the field, HECTOR walks in with a bunch of wildflowers in hand.*

HECTOR: Settin' up the party already?

EVELYN *(playful)*: Hector Johnson, what the hell you doin'?

HECTOR: Lexie come back home, think I'm gonna miss out?

EVELYN: Those are some pretty flowers you got there.

HECTOR: Just flowers from the yard.

EVELYN: Well, we'll need to put them in a vase.

HECTOR: Set them on the table like this… *(He does so)* … look just fine.

EVELYN: Shouldn't have.

HECTOR: Know how Lexie likes her wildflowers. Used to steal them all the time from our yard back in the day. Remember?

EVELYN: Shouldn't have stole.

HECTOR: She was just actin' out. Like all the Glimmer girls.

EVELYN: We are not the-

HECTOR: Like the Glimmer girls. Like the way it sounds. Hell better than Glimord.

EVELYN: It's our name.

HECTOR: People change their names all the time. Look at me. Think my great grand-daddy was a Johnson? Man, he was, like, Gonzalez Huidobro Reyes or somethin'.

EVELYN: Should've kept his name.

HECTOR: Yeah well…back then…it was safer to be a Johnson.

EVELYN: …New aftershave?

HECTOR (playful): Must be my man scent you're smellin'. (a flirtatious caress)

EVELYN: Hector. I got things to do.

HECTOR (caress): You are lookin' fine, Miss Evelyn Jane.

EVELYN: What has gotten into you?

HECTOR: Love you, darlin'.

EVELYN: You're married.

HECTOR: Ain't been home in years.

EVELYN: And if she comes back?

HECTOR: Then I'll ask for divorce. Plain and simple.

EVELYN (*pulling away gently*): Simple for you.

HECTOR: Christ All Mighty, woman, what do you want me to do? I love you.

EVELYN: Not so [loud].

HECTOR: Love you.

EVELYN: …

HECTOR: Evelyn Jane Glimmer.

EVELYN (*perhaps fighting tears*): Quit!

*A moment.*

HECTOR (*gently*): What's goin' on?

EVELYN: World in my head. No where to put it.

HECTOR: Sit yourself down. Rest.

EVELYN: Can't…

HECTOR: A tiny little rest. Breathe. Come on.

*Hector sits. Gestures for her to sit with him.*

*Evelyn sits.*

*A moment between them.*

EVELYN: Lexie should've been here by now.

HECTOR: Maybe she's runnin' late.

EVELYN: …Shouldn't have gone over there in the first place. I told her…

HECTOR: Goes where she's sent, Evelyn. It's orders.

EVELYN: Momma would've never ever let her join up. She knew how to talk to her, make her really think about things. Me and Lexie? I got no way through to her. Never have. Sometimes when we were kids, I used to think I'd been dropped down into this family like ET or somethin'.

HECTOR: Families are what they are. Look at mine, right?

EVELYN: …What's this world come to?

HECTOR: Sorrow. Misery. Bit of healin'.

*ALI walks in with rhubarb pie and some plastic knives and forks in hand.*

ALI *(refers to pie, almost as if it were an announcement)*: Pie's as cool as anythin.'

*Ali sets the pie down on the table along with knives and forks.*

HECTOR: What you got there, Ali?

ALI: Hey. Hector.

EVELYN: Get lost in the house?

ALI: Huh?

EVELYN: Took an awful long time.

ALI *(To Evelyn)*: Act like I'm still in high school.

HECTOR *(refers to pie)*: Looks so good.

EVELYN: Rhubarb pie.

HECTOR: Spoilin' me, girl.

EVELYN: It's not all for you, greedy man.

HECTOR: …just seein' it there…

EVELYN: Don't have to eat it.

HECTOR: Baby, you put pie on a table, I'm gonna eat it.

ALI: Got the gene?

HECTOR: Got the sugar man gene. That's right. (sings, improvising a tune) "Sugar, sugar, sugar man. Love my sugar as best I can."

EVELYN (playful to Hector): So fulla shit.

HECTOR: Hey.

EVELYN: I've seen you have restraint. When you want.

HECTOR: What's she talkin'?

ALI: Don't know.

EVELYN: That chocolate cake I made that time. At the fair.

HECTOR: I was stuffed, honey.

EVELYN: You were lookin' over at that redhead's bake table, eyein' her goods, that's what.

HECTOR: Ali. Help a poor drownin' man.

ALI: Sink away, oh *capitan*!

EVELYN: Look at whomever you want. … At day's end… You're gonna do what all men do.

HECTOR: …What?

EVELYN: Where's the cider, Ali?

HECTOR *(to Evelyn)*: What you talkin'?

ALI: Wasn't there.

HECTOR: Evelyn?

EVELYN: Leave be.

HECTOR: You can't just say somethin' like that and ask me to leave be. What'd you mean by that?

EVELYN: … Men. Do what they do.

HECTOR: Got judgment. Judgment hard in your heart.

EVELYN: Nothin' of the…

HECTOR: Just 'cuz your daddy left doesn't mean-

EVELYN: We are NOT goin' there, y'hear me?! You got no idea what it was like when our daddy left. None at all.

*Brief moment.*

EVELYN (CONT): Now, where's the cider?

ALI: Didn't see it.

EVELYN: Ask for one thing, one thing to be right for this day…

HECTOR: Let it go, baby.

EVELYN: Will you stop it with the "lettin' go?" I know what I want to have on this table when Lexie arrives. If it'd have been up to all of you, she'd have nothin' to come back to.

ALI: Not true.

EVELYN: Like you know anythin'.

ALI: Know what Lexie likes.

EVELYN: You're more of her sister than I am. That your story? 'Cuz last I recall we were ALL in this family. Or did that change all of a sudden?

ALI: Evelyn…

EVELYN: Don't "Evelyn" me. Know the story you like to tell.

ALI: What?

EVELYN: "Oh, my sister's in the war. I'm gonna join her one of these days, be a real hero. " Think I don't hear you talkin'?

ALI: Never said-

EVELYN: Walk round all fake proud…well, listen up, baby: takes as much to stay here, stick it out in this town, than it does to go off, fight in some war we don't even know what for.

HECTOR: Look now, Evelyn…

EVELYN: Look now what? Know 'xactly – Honest to God fact - why Lexie really been sent over there?

HECTOR: Well, not the particulars, but…

EVELYN: Right.

*Evelyn heads toward the house.*

ALI: Where you goin'?

EVELYN: Cider.

*ALEXANDRA (LEXIE) appears in the field, rucksack over her shoulder.*

LEXIE: Y'all fightin' 'bout me already?

ALI: Lexie! Lexie!

*Ali runs to Lexie. Huge embrace.*

*Evelyn walks back. Looks at them.*

LEXIE: Hey, dude, you're all muscle!

ALI: Been workin' out.

LEXIE: Over at the gym?

ALI: Nah. They closed it up. But I go to the schoolyard sometimes and…

LEXIE: Ali the boxer…

ALI: You're the boxer.

LEXIE: Not like you.

ALI: Future Flyweight Champion of the World! That's right!

LEXIE: Give 'em hell, eh?

ALI: Gonna get me in a match one of these days.

LEXIE: Knock 'em out?

ALI & LEXIE *(a phrase they shared once)*: Out and down and into the ground.

LEXIE: Man, it is good to see you.

> *They embrace – fierce, warm, not wanting to let go. Ali is crying.*

LEXIE: Okay.

ALI: Huh?

LEXIE: Okay.

> *Ali lets go. Lexie caresses her hair.*

LEXIE (CONT): I'm here, right?

ALI *(perhaps wiping tears)*: Yeah.

> *A moment.*

EVELYN *(tentative steps forward)*: Hey.

LEXIE: Evelyn.

> *Awkward embrace between them, and then....*

EVELYN: Look good.

LEXIE: Long trip.

EVELYN: Want me to take your bag in?

LEXIE: I'm fine.

*Brief moment.*

EVELYN: What?

LEXIE: Look the same.

EVELYN: You sure your eyes work all right?

LEXIE: [look] Exactly the same.

EVELYN: Don't even recognize myself anymore. Look in the mirror and think "who's that woman?"

*Hector is standing to one side.*

HECTOR: Good to see you, Lexie.

LEXIE: …Hector Johnson? Man, I thought you'd moved away.

HECTOR: No. That was my wife. … *(pointing to…)* Got you them wildflowers. Remember how much you used to like 'em.

LEXIE: Thanks.

LEXIE: …

EVELYN: Flight get in okay?

LEXIE: Bit bumpy, but… it was all right.

EVELYN: Gave the driver the address over the phone. Don't know why he took so long to get you here. Not like the airport's that far out.

LEXIE: Got a ride.

EVELYN: What you mean? We ordered a car to…?

LEXIE: …Met up with Barry…

EVELYN: Barry?

LEXIE: …

EVELYN: We're waitin' here and you GO OFF with Barry…?

LEXIE: Not like that.

EVELYN: We ordered that car. Paid for it to pick you up. Won't get that money back, Lexie. That was pre-paid. Y'hear what I'm sayin'?

LEXIE: …

EVELYN: Sit here all evenin' worried to pieces about you….

ALI (there's history here): …What'd you have?

LEXIE: Just a beer.

*A moment.*

*Lexie looks at table decorations, paper lanterns.*

LEXIE (CONT): Everythin' sure looks nice.

EVELYN: …

LEXIE: What kind of pie is-?

HECTOR: Rhubarb. Evelyn said we couldn't eat it 'til you got here.

ALI: There's cider, buffalo chicken, cole slaw, and baked beans, too.

LEXIE: All that?

EVELYN: For you.

LEXIE: Don't need to…

*EVELYN: Can't have you come back to sandwiches and Coke.

LEXIE: [sound] Just like Momma.

EVELYN: Taught us, didn't she? Taught us what was right.

*Lexie picks up a party favor. Looks at it as if it were a strange object. It is the kind of party favor that makes a sound. She makes a sound with it. The sound hangs in the air.*

*And then…*

EVELYN: Should bring out the cider.

LEXIE: That's all right.

EVELYN: Gotta at least make a toast-

LEXIE: This is all real nice, and that pie looks…

HECTOR: Amazing. Right? When Evelyn gets to cookin'…

LEXIE: Just wanna shower and get some shut-eye.

EVELYN: What?

LEXIE: Long trip. You know?

EVELYN: But Lexie, we got-

*Lexie picks up rucksack.*

LEXIE (CONT): Nice to see you, Hector.

HECTOR: Nice to see you too.

EVELYN *(to Lexie)*: What the hell you talkin' about?

LEXIE: Tired.

EVELYN: And we're waitin' and waitin' all this time while you're... fuckin' Barry?

LEXIE: Huh?

EVELYN:*(refers to pie, etc)* Spent all this on... While the house's goin' to shit, and me workin' this and that odd job,

HECTOR: Evelyn...

EVELYN(*CONT, to Lexie)*: Just so you can come back here, and...

*A moment.*

LEXIE: 'Night, Ali-cakes.

*Ali runs up to her and gives her a quick, strong hug.*

ALI: 'Night.

*Lexie walks away.*

EVELYN: Lexie? I'm talking to you!

*Lexie walks toward the house until she's gone from view.*

*A moment.*

EVELYN (CONT): Well…

HECTOR: …Just like my dad when he came back.

EVELYN: Never served in any war.

HECTOR: Was in the Marines.

EVELYN: In a war in the Marines? … All this pie and…

ALI: We'll eat it later.

EVELYN: Wouldn't even look at me.

HECTOR: 'Course she-

EVELYN: Wouldn't look me in the eye. All this time and she…

*It is clear Evelyn is upset enough to be near tears.*

HECTOR *(draws close)*: Hey.

EVELYN *(walks away)*: Got to clean all this up.

HECTOR: Evelyn.

EVELYN: Ali, help me out here.

ALI: We can leave-

EVELYN: I am NOT leavin' all this mess out here so squirrels can come and make a stink of it.

*Evelyn starts to clear the decorations from the table. Ali helps her.*

HECTOR: Want me to take these lanterns down?

*She hands him back the wildflowers.*

HECTOR (CONT): What are you-?

EVELYN: …

HECTOR: Evelyn.

EVELYN: …

HECTOR: Keep 'em. Cheer up the house.

*He kisses her lightly on the head. Brief moment.*

HECTOR (CONT): Call if you need, all right?

*Evelyn goes back to clearing and cleaning. She sets the pie on one of the chairs, the candle on another.*

HECTOR (CONT): G'night, Ali.

ALI *(midst clearing)*: 'Night.

*He walks away until he is gone from view.*

*The decorations are all cleared, and back in the basket, save for the paper lanterns, which will remain up.*

ALI (CONT): Want me to fold up the tablecloth?

EVELYN *(lost in thought)*: …

ALI: Evelyn?

EVELYN: Huh?

ALI: Tablecloth too?

EVELYN: Leave it.

*Ali picks up basket and starts to walk away.*

EVELYN (CONT): No. Wait. Let's… tablecloth.

*Ali sets the basket down, and grabs one end of the tablecloth, while Evelyn grabs the other. They go about folding it together.*

*ALI: Just like when momma was around.

EVELYN: Hmm?

ALI: When y'all used to fold up the sheets after she'd take them down off the line.

EVELYN: You were nothing but a little itty bitty girl, then. How you remember that?

*ALI: little things…in mind.

EVELYN: … Lexie looked so tired. Like her soul had been drained from her.

*ALI picks up the slack on the folding of the tablecloth and finishes folding it down to size, so that it can fit in the basket with everything else.*

ALI *(CONT, refers to pie and candle on the chairs)*: What you wanna do with the rest of this stuff?

EVELYN: I'll take care of it.

ALI: Don't leave the pie out here.

EVELYN: Girl, you ever seen me leavin' a pie out?

ALI: … Lexie just needs shut-eye. That's all.

EVELYN: …

ALI: She'll be all right.

EVELYN: World is a mess. Downright mess.

*After a brief moment, perhaps during which an affectionate gesture is exchanged between the sisters, Ali heads toward house with basket full of things.*

EVELYN *(calling out)*: Put the wildflowers in a vase, Ali. There's one under the sink from that time.

*Ali walks towards the house until she is gone from view.*

*Evelyn sings an improvised tune to herself, perhaps the same tune she sang earlier.*

*Evelyn looks at the pie and candle. She sets the pie on the table.*

*She picks up the candle, and places it, jar and all, smack down in the center of the pie: a strange, slightly irrational, violent gesture.*

*She blows out the candle.*

*Only the dim light of the paper lanterns is left.*

## Scene Two

*EXT. Night. In the field. It is much later the same evening.*

*The paper lanterns are no longer up. The table and chairs, if still there, are off, to one side, folded up, leaning against a tree or the side of a fence.*

*In the pale moonlight, Lexie is seen. She is in a T-shirt and sweatpants. She boxes with no one. Her fists cut through the air, hard and fast. Quick sharp breaths.*

*She has been at this for a while. Alone. It's just the rush of her body and the unsteady quiet of the night.*

*Jab. Jab. Jab. Punch.*

*The rhythm escalates, as she boxes. Her legs move in the grass and dirt. There is a kind of controlled fury here as Lexie tries to seize the night.*

*A sound in the distance. Odd. Metallic. Perhaps a whistle blowing over at the tobacco farm? Perhaps a bunch of beer cans being tossed onto the road up ahead?*

*Lexie stops. Hyper-aware.*

*No sound now. Just the eerie quiet.*

*She doesn't move. Alert. In position. Ready for anything.*

*And then, confidant in the silence after a little while, she continues boxing, this time with more focus, and even more fury.*

*Jab. Jab. Jab. Punch. Punch.*

*Flurry of punches, one after the other. She is on some kind of weird adrenaline rush now. Her legs dance in the grass and dirt.*

*The moonlight catches her skin. She is pushing herself beyond all reason. Her breathing is quickened, accompanied by a phrase, grunted out...*

LEXIE: If I die in a... If I die in a...

*She keeps boxing, going past the point of any comfort, until all her body can do is fall to the ground, as she sends a holler up into the sky.*

*In the b/g, if the outlines of the simple house are indeed visible, a lone soft light is turned on, a few seconds after the sound of Lexie's holler. Ali calls out from the house:*

ALI (VO): Lexie?

*Lexie does not reply.*

*After slight moment, the light in the house goes dark.*

LEXIE: If I die in a combat zone, box me up and ship me home.

## Scene Three

*EXT. Day. Several weeks later. In the field, Evelyn is seated on a chair. She sews. There is a basket of clothes next to her. She sings a song to keep going.*

### "Where I go"

EVELYN: WHERE I GO, WHERE I GO

NO-WHERE THAT I KNOW;

WHERE I GO, DOWN BELOW

DEEP IN THE RIVER WIDE.


WHERE I GO, EVEN THOUGH

LIGHT BRINGS YONDER TIDE;

WHERE I GO, HEAVEN KNOWS

[THERE'S] A SINNER AT MY SIDE.

*ALI walks out of the house, classifieds section of the local newspaper in hand.*

ALI: That one of Momma's songs?

EVELYN: Yeah.

ALI: Nice.

EVELYN: Just came into my head, that's all.

ALI: Didn't think you'd be up this early.

EVELYN: Should've been up hours ago. Told the Bakers I'd get these alterations in to them by noon. But at the rate I'm goin'…

ALI: Want me to-?

EVELYN: Like you can sew. … Lexie up yet?

ALI: Sleepin'.

EVELYN: All she does. And when it's time for supper, she takes off God knows where. Swear, it's like she's not even back home.

ALI: Give her time.

EVELYN: Hasn't said two words to me since she got back.

ALI: More than that.

EVELYN: Like I'm a piece of furniture.

ALI: Goin' through stuff.

EVELYN: What stuff? [She] tell you anythin'?

ALI: *shakes head*.

EVELYN: (*pricks herself with needle*) Damn needle.

ALI: I'll get the iodine.

EVELYN: Just need to blow on it a bit, let it stabilize.

*She blows on the pricked skin. Ali focuses on the newspaper.*

EVELYN (CONT): Anythin' in them classifieds?

ALI: Lookin'.

EVELYN: Not in high school anymore, baby. Got to find your way.

ALI: Workin' on it.

EVELYN: If you went down to the unemployment office…

ALI: I'll ask Barry for his truck, drive round, see if there's somethin'.

EVELYN: Don't like you hangin' out with Barry and them all.

ALI: …Don't know what you got 'against-

EVELYN: Not against.

ALI: Bet if they were from the same church, you wouldn't bad-talk 'em all the time.

EVELYN: Church got nothin' to do with.

ALI: Is that right?

EVELYN: Look, some people…

ALI: …?

EVELYN: Cut from different cloth, that's all.

ALI: Got same as we do.

EVELYN: Money has nothin' to do-

ALI: Money has EVERYTHIN' to do with.

EVELYN: …They're rough, Ali. Rough people. All right?

ALI: Only way to be, if you wanna live on this earth. Not like we're country club.

EVELYN: Never said-

ALI: I'm the one who worked there in junior high, cleanin' up their napkins, silverware and golf club shit. They will never let us in. Even though our whole family been born here. Right 'cross from those golf courses takin' up space, water and sky from the rest of us.

EVELYN (*mocking, with sense of history*): Carolina gentry.

ALI: Carolina, my ass. All up and down here on Tobacco Road folks are beggin' for a dollar, and those country club shits act like they're the only ones who got a fuckin' RIGHT. … Barry and them all are rough? Well, I'd rather be rough than pretend I'm wearin' some kinda FRONT says the world's okay Glory Hallelujah.

EVELYN: Think I-?

ALI: Sewin' for the Bakers, aren't you?

EVELYN: Need the money.

ALI: And they hire you out 'cuz they're cheap, and they know they can get you cheap.

EVELYN: House is goin' to shit.

ALI: That mean you gotta put up with the Bakers and their-?

EVELYN: Don't see you doin'.

ALI: I'll do…in time.

EVELYN: Sittin' round all summer…

ALI: Nothin' out there.

EVELYN: 'Cuz you don't look.

ALI: Every day.

EVELYN: Dreamin' of boxin' like it's some kinda career.

ALI: Can be.

EVELYN: Ain't real money.

ALI: Give it time…

EVELYN: For you to win some national match somewhere? 'Cuz at the rate you're goin', that ain't gonna happen, if it happens at all-

ALI: I practice.

EVELYN: In a schoolyard.

ALI: …

EVELYN: Can't keep this house on my own, Ali. Place is rottin' from the inside. Got no way to keep it up, if it keeps up. And the mortgage is kickin' us in the ass. If we lose this house, where are we gonna live?

ALI: Sell the land.

EVELYN: What land?

ALI: Here.

EVELYN: This here's a patch. Somebody come 'round, piss in it. That's all they do.

ALI: Lexie will help out. Been helpin'-

EVELYN: Don't you talk to me 'bout her.

ALI: We'll ALL help out.

EVELYN: I got ten fuckin' little jobs, and they don't add up to one.

ALI: If you worked at the tobacco-

EVELYN: RJ Reynolds and the rest of them can kiss my ass, [if] they think I'm gonna do what Momma done, and work tobacco all my life. ... I sew for the fuckin' Bakers 'cuz I have to. And I'll sew and clean for the Ashfords and McCormicks too. 'Cuz it's either me, or twenty other people in this town who'll do the same. And those twenty other people will run right over me to get the job. And they won't care WHAT. Wanna talk 'bout "rough?" "Rough" ain't some dream, Ali, of trucks and boxin' and gettin' drunk til three AM...

ALI: I'll get us some money, all right!

EVELYN: Staggerin' outta the bar with the boys after ten games of pool and however many ounces of beer and whisky. Think I don't know that dream you play out with Barry and them all about joinin' up and-?

ALI: ...

EVELYN: Was gonna be me and Sean, right?

ALI: Always with that-

EVELYN: Don't you disrespect me, baby girl. Me and Sean were gonna get married,

ALI: …

EVELYN: Were gonna turn this land over, do all sorts of things. 'Cept Sean got himself killed over there in that war you wanna go to so much, 'cuz whatever Lexie does, you wanna do too.

ALI: Not like that…

EVELYN: Had fuckin' plans. Big ol fuckin' plans. Just like you got no plans 'cept to look through them classifieds every mornin' like some job gonna spring up from the paper like magic.

ALI: That what you-?

EVELYN: What I see, girl. Or do you think just 'cuz my eyes ain't workin' right I don't see nothin'?

ALI: …

EVELYN: When I go blind as batshit, you can go round, do whatever. But until then… I promised Momma…I'd do right by you and all of us. And if that means suckin' it up to the Bakers and anyone else that gives me a job to keep this house and put some kind of food on the table, you better fuckin' believe I'm gonna play that stupid little game until it hurts. And if you wanna cry "Oh Evelyn's such a bad sister, such a mean, bad big ol' sister," go on. Cry all you want. 'Cuz I know what we're tryin' to have here is a decent life - somethin' Barry and them all know nothin' 'bout.

ALI: …Fulla shit.

EVELYN: What?

ALI: You go round all high and mighty, but when Lexie shipped out, I remember you prayin' to all the saints in heaven that she stay there a long time.

EVELYN: I never-

ALI: Wanted her gone. Far, far away, 'cuz you hated she always did better than you.

EVELYN: Huh?

ALI: She'd win some prize at school? You'd be all weirded-out. She made a real decision with her life? You didn't know what to do with. 'Cuz she's just like Daddy. Lexie is just like Daddy and Daddy was a piece of shit.

EVELYN: Never said…

ALI: Piece of shit for leavin' us, piece of shit 'cuz Momma got sick after he left, piece of shit it was his fault she up and died, 'cuz if he hadn't left, maybe she wouldn't have gotten sick in the first place -

EVELYN: That's not what I-

ALI: And Lexie got his eyes and Lexie got his spirit and Lexie a soldier too, and that just puts you out like hellfire. But you know what? Lexie's more than you. Come Day of Judgment? Book gonna show she done right. And you, with all the powerful decency you say you got – Nobody's gonna remember you. Nobody's gonna say "Oh that Evelyn, she's a golden child." Your name drop in the bucket? Good riddance. That's what people will say. Nobody but nobody's gonna sing at your grave.

*Evelyn strikes Ali.*

43

EVELYN: Sorry, ungrateful child. Earth gonna swallow you up, and there won't be anythin' I can do when you cry out.

ALI: Fuck you.

EVELYN: Ali.

ALI: Fuck you to hell.

*Ali runs off.*

EVELYN: Ali?!

*Ali is gone.*

*A moment.*

*Lexie walks out of the house.*

LEXIE: Just like the ol' days.

EVELYN: Thought you were-

LEXIE: With your racket goin' on?

*Evelyn picks up basket.*

LEXIE (CONT): [is] That laundry you got there?

EVELYN: Work.

LEXIE: Who for?

EVELYN: Work's work. We can't all sit 'round here, lookin' up at the sky.

*LEXIE draws a cigarette from pack in her pocket.*

EVELYN (CONT): Thought you quit.

LEXIE: Breakfast.

EVELYN: Can't live on tobacco.

LEXIE: Whole town does. Got off the plane, could smell it hangin' in the air, followin' me 'round like "Come on, maggot, light up."

*She lights up.*

EVELYN: Get you juice.

LEXIE: Don't want.

EVELYN: Need somethin' besides-

LEXIE: I'll get, if I want.

EVELYN: … All right.

*Evelyn heads toward the house.*

LEXIE: Where'd Ali go?

EVELYN: …Don't know. Don't know what she does anymore.

*Evelyn walks toward the house, with basket and newspaper, until she is gone from view. Lexie smokes. She looks at the sky.*

LEXIE: Strange weather comin' down foul n' beautiful.

*She jabs at the air.*

LEXIE (CONT, *talkin' to the sky*): Strange weather, gonna beat me down?

*She jabs at the air. Brief flurry. Followed by a laugh and perhaps a short cough. She takes a drag on the cigarette, and then... she recalls an army cadence call.*

### "The Yellow Bird"

LEXIE (CONT): A YELLOW BIRD,
WITH A YELLOW BILL,
WAS SITTIN' ON
MY WINDOW SILL.
I LURED HIM IN
WITH A CRUST OF BREAD
AND THEN I SMASHED
HIS FUCKIN' HEAD.

*She laughs, perhaps a little too much (out of anger and bitterness?). Evelyn walks out of the house with two mugs of coffee in hand.*

EVELYN: Singin'?

LEXIE *(making it up)*: Air.

EVELYN: That right?

LEXIE: Noisy.

EVELYN *(playing along)*: Cackle of birds, eh?

LEXIE: Chirp chirp.

EVELYN: *(holding out coffee mug)* Here.

LEXIE: Said I didn't...

EVELYN: Just coffee. For God's sake.

*Lexie sips coffee.*

LEXIE: Sweet.

*Lexie sets down coffee mug on the ground, and smokes.*

EVELYN: Shouldn't smoke.

LEXIE *(a joke)*: Let me die young, oh Lord.

EVELYN: Quit.

LEXIE: Come on, Evelyn.

EVELYN: No. Don't like that.

LEXIE: Wanna smoke, okay? Wanna fill up my lungs with nicotine just like Daddy done.

EVELYN: Don't even know where he is.

LEXIE: Smokin' somewhere, I bet. Free n' easy.

*A moment.*

LEXIE (CONT): Got work?

EVELYN: Alterations day.

LEXIE *(slightly mocking)*: Pick-ups and deliveries.

EVELYN: Some folks got nothin'.

LEXIE: …Don't know why people alter anythin'. Just as easy to get somethin' at the store.

EVELYN: The pieces I work on are vintage.

LEXIE: Like, from last year?

EVELYN: Quit.

LEXIE: Gonna go blind…

EVELYN: I'm fine.

*A moment.*

EVELYN (CONT): Sleep okay?

LEXIE: Quiet.

EVELYN *(insinuating)*: Good whisky?

LEXIE *(takes a brief moment, and then fesses up and embellishes)*: …Yeah. It was good. Right from the still, too.

EVELYN: … Gonna stay for supper tonight?

LEXIE: That what this is about: coffee, breakfast, sit out here…?

EVELYN: Just askin'.

LEXIE: … Can't eat anymore.

EVELYN: …?

LEXIE: Nothin' tastes like anythin'.

EVELYN: When'd this-?

LEXIE: Long time.

EVELYN: … Seen Army doc 'bout?

LEXIE: With all the crazy shit goin' on down there in that sandbox, you think they got time to deal with whether I got any chow or not? As long as I was doin' my job...

EVELYN: See one here, then. Can't live on whisky and cigarettes.

LEXIE: I'll be fine.

EVELYN: Can't let things go on...

LEXIE: What things?

EVELYN: Remember when you had that infection that time...

LEXIE: I was eight years old, Evelyn. That was a helluva long time ago.

EVELYN: Well...

LEXIE: No use worryin'.

EVELYN: Who else am I gonna worry about? Between you and Ali...

LEXIE: Leave Ali alone.

EVELYN: Got no direction in life.

LEXIE: She'll find it. Just gotta leave her be and not get all in her shit.

EVELYN: I don't-

LEXIE: She's not a kid, Evelyn. Can't cuss her out and put fear of God in her like she's a kid, all right?

EVELYN: … Barry say somethin' to you?

LEXIE: What's Barry got to-?

EVELYN: Seein' Barry, aren't you?

LEXIE: Fuck me.

EVELYN (CONT, *over*): That's where you go, isn't it? Out all night and join Ali in her escapades.

LEXIE: Escapades?

EVELYN: You. Go. Out.

LEXIE: You know, I should leave. Get my own place.

EVELYN: This is your home.

LEXIE: This is where I grew up, it's not my home.

EVELYN: … If you wanna see that man…

LEXIE: We talk, that's all. We go back.

EVELYN: Back so far you see him before you come back to us? You and Ali, always do what you want.

LEXIE: Evelyn.

EVELYN: Always the one who has to put up with ALL the shit.

LEXIE: What the hell-?

EVELYN: Who do you think it was [that] had to keep it all goin', bills paid on time, house halfway in order, when you were over there doin' your duty?

LEXIE: Doin' cuz…

EVELYN: Yeah. We all heard. And we all heard they were sendin' soldiers back home too, not keepin' on sendin' them over.

LEXIE: Don't know a thing.

EVELYN: They didn't send you over, when they swore left and right, up and down, that ALL THAT over there was nearly done and put to rest?

LEXIE: …

EVELYN: Well, I'm gonna talk to those recruitment officers, then. 'Cuz they straight up and lied to me, lied to all of us.

LEXIE: Get sent where they need.

EVELYN: Some, not others.

LEXIE: Huh?

EVELYN: If we were country club, sure as hell they would've needed you closer to home.

LEXIE: Gonna start with-?

EVELYN: Or off to Europe somewhere livin' the life.

LEXIE: Country club wouldn't even join up.

EVELYN: 'Xactly. Get sent NOT where they need, but where they know they can use you up. Like Momma used to say "The poor ain't nothin' but cannon fodder."

LEXIE: Momma didn't mean-

EVELYN: And all the while who's standin' here, holdin' down the fort? Dollar store bread and corn oil make a good sandwich, you think? 'Cuz that's what Ali and I lived on for weeks.

LEXIE: Got Mickey D's and-

EVELYN: Mickey D's shit. We'd still be livin' on, if I hadn't invented ten little jobs outta nothin' just to keep up.

LEXIE: I sent-

EVELYN: Got leaky roof, plumbin' needs fixin', whole house deterioratin' before my eyes...

LEXIE: I sent enough for-

EVELYN: Mortgage pay itself?

LEXIE: ... Okay.

EVELYN: Go on. Walk away. Just like Ali. Can't face the shit.

LEXIE: Where the hell you think I've been?

EVELYN: ...

LEXIE: Drivin fuckin' Humvee like I'm goin' out for a ride to Myrtle Beach for a bit of sun and surf down me tequila call it a day?

EVELYN: Ain't said-

LEXIE: Like you know anythin' 'bout anythin'.

EVELYN: Understand you got-

LEXIE: If you UNDERSTAND so much, then what the hell you're on me 'bout? *(mimicking Evelyn's tone of voice)* Smokin' this,

smokin' that. *(and then)* Man, I wanna burn myself up. Take a cig, put it 'gainst my skin and so long, world.

EVELYN: … Lexie …

LEXIE: [I] Get back, nothin' but eye-ballin' me all the time.

EVELYN: I'm not-

LEXIE: Itchin' for me to get a job.

EVELYN: Need to get into swing of things.

LEXIE: Swing of what? Ice cream stand?

EVELYN: …There's no talkin'-

LEXIE: There is talkin'. Yeah. But behind all the talkity talk, I see you lookin' at me with your "good intentions." Hell with good intentions. They'll end you up in the latrine every time.

EVELYN: That's not what-

LEXIE: Well then, must be somebody else who CAN'T FACE THE SHIT.

EVELYN: All right now.

LEXIE: Gonna wake Hector and the other neighbors, ruin their mornin'?

EVELYN: Hector don't-

LEXIE: Oh. Right. He's workin' already. Gotta sell cars to the five people who got real money in this town.

EVELYN: Hector's a good man.

LEXIE: Fuck who you want.

EVELYN: I don't sleep with-

LEXIE: Why not? Loves you.

EVELYN: ...How you-?

LEXIE: Clear as day, just from lookin' at how he looks at you.

EVELYN: What Hector and I have-

LEXIE: Look, you want me to stick 'round for supper? This what ALL THIS is about? Want me to sit, make like everythin's normal? Okay. I'll be normal. I'll do it.

EVELYN: Lexie.

LEXIE: I'll do as you say, ma'am. Yes, ma'am. Whatever you say, ma'am. *(falling into an Army cadence):*

## "Bodies, Bodies, Bodies"[1]

LEXIE (CONT): ANYTHING FOR YOU,
ANYTHING YOU TELL ME TO,
'CAUSE ALL I EVER WANT TO SEE
ARE BODIES, BODIES, BODIES.

---

[1] This Army cadence historically is sung to the tune of the 1950s Teresa Brewer pop-country hit "(Put Another Nickel In) Music Music Music."

EVELYN: …

LEXIE: Tell me a story from way back.

EVELYN: Lexie…

LEXIE: Tell me a story 'bout chicks that try to fly out of the coop, and get smashed to bits by the big hen that lays runny eggs at night, and stuffs them down the little chicks' throats, 'cuz all they have is the run run run of those rotten eggs, and all they can do is pray their smashed little bits don't get scattered over too much of the sweaty earth, 'cuz if they don't stay together, even in bits, they won't know who they are, or why they were put on this earth to begin with.

EVELYN: That was Momma's story.

LEXIE: But she made sure she told it to you, so you could re-tell it to all of us. She made sure we knew we had nothin, and that we were never gonna have. So that when we played at being "normal," we knew full well what we were playin' at.

EVELYN: Didn't mean it like that.

LEXIE: You ask her? On her deathbed?

EVELYN: …She gave us songs and stories to get through...

LEXIE: And what we get through? What fuckin' mess [did] we get through?

EVELYN: … Look, all I meant-

LEXIE: Sent money over. Much more than I ever could've made if I'd stuck it out here in this town.

EVELYN: All right.

LEXIE: All right nothin'. Think I wanted to go over there to the stink n' shit? Think I had some kinda choice? I'm a POG.[2] Plain and simple. Bitch ho dyke POG from nowhere.

EVELYN: You're not-

LEXIE: That's what they called me, called all of us. (*as a sergeant's order*) Bitch ho dyke, get down, and give me ten.

*As an Army cadence:*

LEXIE (CONT): Bitch ho dyke from ol' town Sodom, strike matches on her bottom.
*And then...*

LEXIE (CONT): Or you think just 'cuz Daddy served, they'd give me special privilege? Daddy was a POG too. So, whatever dream you got in your head...

EVELYN: No dream. I just...

LEXIE: I talk to Barry cuz yeah, he's easy. We drink. Shoot the shit. Doesn't ask me about anythin'. And I don't ask him 'bout what he does or how many kids he got from all the different women he's had. It's simple. I want simple now. ... Not that that's somethin' you'd understand. 'Cuz you want close and in your face and oh let's be out here and think about how good everythin' is in this country.

---

[2] POG military term for person other than grunt. That is what infantry call women, air wingers, logisticians, motor transportation drivers (which was Lexie's role).

EVELYN: I know things-

LEXIE: You ACT like you got rage and fierceness inside you. You tear into Ali, 'cuz she's so easy to tear into -She's a baby doll she's that easy - And you twist that knife, and you make her twist it too, until both of you are sayin' things you shouldn't be sayin' over some JOB that ain't even out there, and ain't ever gonna be out there ever again. And here I am, right in the thick of it, right in the four-feet-down-in-the-ground head-throbbin' mess of it, and all you care 'bout is whether I stay for supper?

EVELYN: That's not what I-

LEXIE: Supper gonna make everythin' go away, Evelyn? Supper gonna heal like some preacher at church?

Oh mighty the ground we walk on when we profess our healin' to an earth that can't listen no more, 'cuz it is busted-up and weary and sick-fast and hungry.

EVELYN *(gently)*: Lexie...

LEXIE: Think I sleep? Sleep and sleep all through the day? I never sleep. There is no shut-eye to speak of. I lie in that bed up there in the house under that fuckin' ceilin' full of water stains, and I stare. Hard. Thinkin' of nothin' and everythin'.

And when you're all hushed or pretendin' to be, I slip out, yeah. Not for a goddamn "escapade." No, ma'am. I run, past the dogwoods and the mess of snakes and the heat that gathers in the old barns, and I find some spot somewhere that feels lost and stinky and beat to shit, and I hide in a muscle of water all night, sweatin', shiverin' and full of shame.

So, don't you be tellin' me what you think I'm doin' or not doin', or how I should be behavin' to help you feel better about the goddamn mess we're ALL in here, there, and everywhere anyone calls home.

Light shines in the distance, but what I see ain't no light. No, ma'am. What I see's fire, pure achin', and it's gonna rage all over this here earth, until we got nothin' but to hold on hard close, and hope we ain't ash before mornin'.

## Scene four

*EXT. Evening. Much later the same day. The basket of clothes is gone, as is the newspaper.*

*Evelyn lays a blanket out in the field. From her pockets she adorns the blanket with small twigs: a ritual. As she does so, she sings a song without words: a call to the heavens. The song has the quality of an old mountain song (born of old Scottish ballads).*

*In the b/g, there may be occasional flashes of lightning in the sky. The threat of rain, but no visible signs yet.*

### "Song without words"

EVELYN: OO, AH, EE, AH, OO.

OO, AH, EE, AH, OO.

> *Breath.*

> *The melody builds and transforms…*

OO, AH, EE, AH, OO, AH, EE, OH…

> *Slight breath.*

OO, AH, EE, AH, OO.

> *Breath.*

*She repeats the entire vocal sequence above again, and then…*

*She looks at the pattern of twigs upon the blanket. Hector walks in from another part of the field. He looks at her.*

HECTOR: Whatcha doin' out here, woman?

EVELYN: Somethin' Momma used to [do]. Whenever we got lost.

HECTOR: How's a blanket with twigs got anythin' to do with gettin' lost?

EVELYN: Said it'd find us.

HECTOR: Huh?

EVELYN: By lookin' at it. Said the way the twigs get laid out show a trail, the way back home. Ali's lost. This could find her.

HECTOR: Lexie'll bring her back.

EVELYN: What if she don't?

HECTOR: Can't be gone that far.

EVELYN: Then how come she ain't been found yet? Should be out there.

HECTOR: I looked, all right? Lexie's keepin' on. She's got better sense of these things, anyway.

EVELYN: What things?

HECTOR: Search and rescue kind of things. Now, come on, put all this mess away.

EVELYN: Leave it.

HECTOR: Gonna rain, woman. You're gonna sit out here in the rain?

EVELYN: Sit here 'til she comes back.

HECTOR: Christ All Mighty, the day I met you…

EVELYN: Don't have to stay, Hector. Ain't obligatin'.

*HECTOR: What good's it do me to go back home when I know you're sittin' out here? I'll just be thinkin' about you all the time.

*He sits next to her. They look at the blanket.*

*A moment.*

HECTOR (CONT): Is it some kinda Indian thing?

EVELYN: Just somethin' Momma would do.

HECTOR: …What you think twigs say?

EVELYN: Don't know.

HECTOR: Can't you read them?

EVELYN: Momma never taught me how.

HECTOR: I bet if we look at it, we could figure it out. Where'd you start?

EVELYN *(points to area on blanket)*: Over here.

HECTOR: Here's home?

EVELYN: I guess.

HECTOR: So, if this is where Ali was, and… *(looks at pattern on blanket)* she went there… That's north, right?

EVELYN: From that angle.

HECTOR: Let's say north. So, if she went north, and then... *(looks at pattern on blanket)* went over here... what would this be?

EVELYN: East?

HECTOR: ...Ocean?

EVELYN: If she went east and kept on goin'.

HECTOR: That'd be too far.

EVELYN: Don't know, then.

HECTOR:*(looks at next pattern)* What about this?

EVELYN: That's nothin'.

HECTOR: What you mean?

EVELYN: Arbitrary.

HECTOR: Laid these twigs down. How can they be arbitrary? There's always a reason, right?

EVELYN: Logic. Yeah.

HECTOR: So, if there's logic, what's this?

EVELYN: *(looks, then)* Back north?

HECTOR: Back toward these parts. So, she's close. Be here in no time.

EVELYN: ...Sure believe awful fast.

HECTOR: Goin' by the signs, Evelyn.

EVELYN: What if the signs are wrong?

HECTOR: ...?

EVELYN: What if all them twigs mean nothin' but just plain ol' wishful-ness?

HECTOR: Then I take the wishful-ness in my hands and send it up to heaven, have it send me a sign.

EVELYN: Just like that?

HECTOR: Just like.

*SFX: Wee crack of thunder.*

HECTOR (CONT): See? What'd I tell you?

EVELYN: Rain.

HECTOR: Rain comin'. That's right.

EVELYN: Rain don't mean she'll be back.

HECTOR: If you don't believe in anythin', Evelyn, then why'd you do all this?
EVELYN: *shrugs.*

HECTOR: Ali wouldn't just up and leave, and not come back.

EVELYN: After what I said...

HECTOR: If I were to take to heart everythin' you ever said to me or anyone ever said to me... I'd be whole other country by now.

EVELYN: ...Don't think I've ever met anyone like you.

HECTOR (*flirtatious*): That's 'cuz there isn't. I'm the one and only. Hector Johnson.

EVELYN: Quit.

HECTOR (*gently*): Come on, Evelyn. How long we been through this? We're meant for each other, baby. Ever since that day…

EVELYN: What day?

HECTOR: Came on over to the dealership to look at the cars…

EVELYN: …

HECTOR: Had that pretty yellow dress on. The one with the flowers.

EVELYN: Don't have a yellow-

HECTOR: Got flowers on it. Little tiny flowers. Daisies or dandelions or somethin'.

EVELYN: Dandelions ain't flowers.

HECTOR: And you were lookin' at all the SUV's, tryin' to make up your mind. Bright, sunny day. And you said to me, "Got anythin' with a stick?" And I was like, "First woman walk into my lot lookin' for somethin' with a stick." And you just smiled and… There were sparks. Like my whole body was like them little bits of lightnin' flickerin' up there in that sky.

EVELYN: Can't afford an SUV.

HECTOR: I'm telling you, we looked at each other. And I said to myself, "I'm gonna be with this woman my whole life. Until we're old and smelly and makin' a mess of ourselves."

EVELYN: Hector…

HECTOR: Want to, Evelyn. Ever since that day…

EVELYN (*softly, with a caress perhaps*): Can't, baby.

*A moment.*

HECTOR: You know, what Lexie gone through…

EVELYN: And what Sean gone through, and what Daddy and Momma gone through, and what Ali's goin' through – you think all this stuff just goes away? Think all this family shit just vanishes like some storybook story? I was eighteen years old when Momma passed. And ever since that day, it's ALL, ALL been on me.

HECTOR: Can't live your-

EVELYN: Somebody's got to have some sense 'round here. Even if-

*Evelyn is at a loss for a moment, and then she starts gathering all the twigs quickly. He tries to stop her.*

HECTOR: Evelyn…

EVELYN: Leave me alone.

*Evelyn has an ungainly bunch of twigs in her hands. She is trying to contain them all. She is fighting tears, but is not letting herself release.*

HECTOR: Hey now.

*Hector draws close. She is trembling. He touches her hands gently and begins to unburden her of the twigs.*

*She embraces him. Twigs fall every which way to the ground and upon the blanket.*

*They are in the embrace for a long time.*

*And then, they look at each other. He caresses her hair. She caresses his face.*

EVELYN: Want everythin' to be...

HECTOR: Sometimes, you gotta let the mess just be what it is.

*They go about picking up the twigs and putting them back in the basket.*

HECTOR (CONT): Where'd you get all these damn twigs, anyway? Ain't steal them from my yard, did you?

EVELYN: Like I got reason to go sneakin' 'round your yard-

HECTOR: Glimmer girls always done.

EVELYN: Quit with that.

HECTOR *(singing to her, improvising a tune, riffing)*: Glimmer glimmer, glimmer Jane. Evelyn Glimmer, queen of-.

*He is interrupted by SFX: flash of lightning, followed by crack of thunder.*

HECTOR (CONT): Holy shit.

*Evelyn reaches for the blanket. A sudden rain drenches them.*

HECTOR: Crap.

> *Evelyn laughs, as it keeps raining.*

HECTOR (CONT): Think it's funny now?

EVELYN: [you're] Like one of them cartoon characters.

HECTOR: Give me that blanket.

*She half-gives blanket to him, he half-wrests it from her. He tries to cover them with the blanket.*

EVELYN *(laughs)*: It's all wet.

> *After slight moment, she stands apart, in the rain.*

HECTOR (CONT): What are you doin'?

EVELYN *(in her own world)*: Don't care about anythin'.

HECTOR: Let's go to the house.

EVELYN: …

HECTOR: Come on. I'll race you.

EVELYN *(quoting something she heard once in childhood)*:
And the rain came, and the sky cried, and the whole world looked up at the gods of anger and asked them why, and no one answered. No one at all.

HECTOR *(fighting rain)*: What are you-?

EVELYN (*between herself and the world*): Even the rain came down hard and black and strong as tobacco.

HECTOR: Evelyn?

> *Evelyn kisses Hector. A deep, lingering kiss.*

> *SFX: The rain begins to stop.*

HECTOR (CONT): Would you look at that? Rain's stoppin'.

EVELYN: Y'know how it gets in summer.

HECTOR (*flirtatious*): Know how you get in summer.

EVELYN: Now now...

HECTOR: What?

EVELYN: Need to... stop all this.

HECTOR: Why? 'Cuz Lexie and Ali and-?

EVELYN: Everythin'.

> *Brief moment, and then he takes off his shirt.*

EVELYN: Hector!

HECTOR: Soaked through n through. Don't matter much anymore.

> *He draws close to her.*

EVELYN: Whatcha doin'?

HECTOR: Nothin.'

*A moment between them.*

HECTOR *(CONT, intimate)*: What?

EVELYN: If I ever marry you…

HECTOR: Yeah?

EVELYN: Gotta do it right.

HECTOR: Won't let you down, baby. We'll do a nice party with streamers and-

EVELYN: Don't want a fuss.

HECTOR: Whatever you want.

EVELYN: A cake would be nice, though.

HECTOR: Then we'll get a big ol' cake made special.

EVELYN: …Your chest smells of rain… and donuts.

HECTOR: Startin' to get fat.

EVELYN: All that sugar, sugar man.

*It is clearing now. There may even be a slightly freakish crisp light in the evening sky. Lexie walks in from another part of the field.*

LEXIE: Sonofabitch rain. Where'd it come from?

HECTOR *(playful)*: From the moon.

LEXIE: Huh?

EVELYN: Any sign of Ali?

LEXIE: Was seen over at Hog's Den.

EVELYN: What the-?

HECTOR (to Evelyn): Bar. Way the hell over other side of town.

EVELYN: How'd she-?

LEXIE: Ain't there, though.

EVELYN: Checked?

LEXIE: Been everywhere. Barry and them all were lookin' too.  Man, when are you gonna get the truck fixed?

EVELYN: Ali took off with somebody over at that Hog-?

HECTOR: Hog's Den.

EVELYN: She take off with-?

LEXIE: No. Not that anybody'd seen. Gotta get something dry on.

EVELYN: Should keep lookin'.

LEXIE: Been lookin'.

EVELYN: She out there somewhere, you're gonna give up? … Some soldier.

LEXIE: Don't you get in my face. Been hours, right? While you here, waitin' it out. Your mess to begin with.

EVELYN: What?

HECTOR: I should go.

LEXIE: Days and days makin' her feel like shit.

EVELYN: One day I-

LEXIE: And all them other times? They don't count? Man, you think my mind turned to jelly over there in that sandbox?

HECTOR: These things…

LEXIE: These things what, Hector? Got opinions now about who we are, what we've been through?

EVELYN: Don't talk to him like-

LEXIE: Talk how I like.

EVELYN: Every hour that you-

LEXIE: Every hour counts. Yeah. Think I'm not cognizant? - Like that word? Big word, huh? – Somebody goes AWOL? Every fuckin' second counts. I've been cognizant from zero hour on. *(walking away)*

HECTOR: Listen up, there's no need to get all-

LEXIE: What you gonna call me on? 'Least I done somethin' in my life, not sit here in this town complainin' about my little heart murmur so as not to join up.

HECTOR: You're outta pocket now.

LEXIE: Well, I'd rather be outta pocket than sit on my ass sellin' cars to the Bakers and all them that cut us out of any kind of decent livin' in this-

EVELYN: Cut the shit.

LEXIE: What shit? What kind of shit is this that you make Ali run away from her own home, when she's the only thing, only goddamn fuckin' hope we got in this world? … Man, I look and look, and this earth speak to me in no kind of tongue, 'cept the tongue of sickness.

*Lexie heads back to the house when she is stopped by a rustle in the field. Ali appears, fists clenched, but smiling. Her clothes are messed up. She has bruises on her face. She is bleeding a bit from her left eyebrow.*

LEXIE (CONT): Ali?

ALI: Won.

EVELYN: What?

ALI: I. Won.

*Ali opens her fists. They are full of multiple denominations of dollar bills. Although she is exhausted physically, she tosses the bills into the air with laughter in a gesture of victory.*

*Lights fade. End of Part One.*

# Part Two

## Scene Five

*EXT. Night. A little bit later the same evening. On the back porch, Lexie tends to Ali's bruises.*

ALI: Hurts.

LEXIE: Think boxin's just some game? If you wanna do this, it's gonna hurt all the time, Ali-cakes.

ALI: Won, though.

LEXIE: Shouldn't have gone all the way out there.

ALI: Prize money.

LEXIE: Don't need-

ALI: Yes, we do. Need to fix the house, get a job, get some save-up money back in the bank, get you a job, find new house if we can't-

LEXIE: Hey. Slow the hell down, soldier.

ALI: ... Need.

*Brief moment.*

LEXIE: Should go back to school.

ALI: No good at it.

LEXIE: College. Make somethin' of yourself.

ALI: I'm not like you.

LEXIE: ...

ALI: You're a hero, dude. *(reacts to ointment Lexie puts on eyebrow cut)*

LEXIE: Hold still.

ALI: Hurts.

LEXIE: Next time put Vaseline on your eyebrows. Protect them. What'd you think the pro boxers do?

ALI: Guy at the bar was so freaked out when I said I wanted to fight. Thought I was nothin' but a baby doll and would break at nothin'. I showed them. Showed them all.

LEXIE: What'd you show?

ALI: Stuff.

LEXIE: Got the stuff?

ALI: Yeah.

LEXIE *(army cadence)*: Lock and load my M-16,

Show the world I'm lean and mean.

ALI: Hell yeah.

LEXIE: Don't need to go out to some bar way out there off the edge of the tobacco road to show some shitfaced sonofabitch you got the stuff.

ALI: Wasn't like that.

LEXIE: Could've gotten hurt big-time. That wadn't no regulation fight.

ALI: Sound just like Evelyn.

LEXIE: Well, she's right. Can't go 'round doin' this kinda stuff.

ALI: Don't go 'round-

LEXIE: Some asshole wanna beat you to shit, leave you for dead, who's gonna look out for you? Barman will toss your body out, put you in dumpster and nobody will know about anythin' 'bout anythin' if someone come 'round and ask.

ALI: Made us three hundred dollars. (*pulls away.*)

LEXIE (*refers to tending to her bruises*): Not finished.

ALI: Help us fix the roof.

LEXIE: Still don't mean you can-

ALI: Can't show up after being gone all this time, and tell me what to do. If I wanna fight, I'll fight.

LEXIE: Who for?

ALI: …?

LEXIE: Who you fighting for?

ALI: …I'm good.

LEXIE: Then work on it. In a gym.

ALI: Closed down.

LEXIE: Then, find another. Do it right. No sense puttin' yourself someplace where you can get yourself killed.

ALI: You did.

LEXIE: … Come here.

ALI: …

LEXIE: Ali.

Ali: *sits.*

LEXIE: …Every day I was over there, anythin' could've happened. But I didn't go in, askin' for…

ALI: …

LEXIE: Understand?

ALI: …

LEXIE: Look, you walk into some shit bar in the middle of bumfuck and beg some barman for a fight-

ALI: Didn't' beg.

LEXIE: you are committin' outright suicide.

ALI: …

LEXIE: Ain't got much faith left, ain't like Evelyn, but you oughta thank God and all the angels in heaven they were lookin' out for you tonight.

ALI: Just wanted…

LEXIE *(heard it before)*: Do things. Big important things.

ALI: Just money.

LEXIE: Sometimes the world is spinnin' so much, you feel like you gotta cut through it somehow just to keep goin'.

ALI: …

LEXIE: Think I don't know? Think every wakin' minute I was over there I didn't feel that? Think I don't feel it every second I'm here?

ALI: …

LEXIE: Evelyn may have wanted a party, but there was no one else doin' any kind of parade when I come back. It's not like there were miles and miles of yellow ribbons. No one even wants to talk about what's really happenin' over there, not even Barry, 'cuz the further away, the more invisible it is, the better. *(imagining what people may say)* "Keep that war and what's goin' on away from me, citizen. Don't wanna hear me any miserable shit. Got 'nough at home."

Well, it all may be invisible-ness to them, but we're here, right? All of us that went over… all of us that made it back… we're right here. "Ain't just about the money." Like Momma used to say.

ALI: Yeah?

LEXIE: Listen, when me and Evelyn were little, and you were just a whiny speck of a girl.

ALI: I wasn't-

LEXIE: When you were a little girl? Dude, you were whiny.

ALI: …

LEXIE: Momma would sit us out here lookin' out into a night that looked more like a pane of indigo glass than anythin' else, and she'd tell us stuff 'bout when she was a girl, and she worked over at the tobacco farm.

LEXIE: Said sometimes she was so tired at the end of the day that her ankles would just give way, and she'd fall straight upon the earth, inside its whispery sound, and lie there for hours thinkin': if there was any place worse than where she was, then somebody was gonna have to show it to her, because she couldn't imagine anythin' worse than this here sweet Carolina.

Then she'd put her fingers to her cracked lips, dry from the blisterin' heat, and find a way to get up and go on to the shack at the far edge of the farm where her people were waitin' for her, as the sun sunk into smoke.

And don't you know they were as tired as she was? They were bone tired, and full of hurt, and weird joint pains, and fingers curled up from stretchin' and pullin' the tobacco leaves, and they didn't want to hear anythin' 'bout her tiredness, 'cuz hers was girl hurt, and girl hurt has a way of passin'. But grown-up hurt? Grown-up hurt is like a fire lickin' your soul, and it don't pass no-how. It stays with you, and you gotta figure out how you're gonna make it LOOK like it's passin'.

Momma said she'd sit there in the shack, on a thin itchy rag of a mattress, and listen to their stories. Regular stories 'bout how much they'd made that day, and how much they were gonna send back to their kin, and how blessed it was that this place existed, 'cuz if somebody didn't want tobacco somewhere, then they wouldn't have a job.

She said hearin' those stories, made her feel like, even if she was a girl, and she really shouldn't be workin' in the fields at all, -Why, she should playin' basketball or goin' to school or somethin'- knowin' there was some kind of purpose to life felt good.

We'd say Momma, but how could you think such a thing? How could you stay in that smelly place, and not wanna burn it the hell down?

She'd look at us, and smile at your squishy little baby girl face, and say: We all find ourselves our own baptism. We all get through what we get through, even if no one's hangin' any kind of flag for us. Ain't just about the money. And then she'd make up a little song, and sing us right to sleep.

*Lexie sings to Ali.*

**"Born to burn"**

LEXIE (CONT): ALL OF US ARE BORN TO BURN;

BORN ALONG THE WAY.

SUDDEN FLASH OF WEARY BIRDS

SHOW US LIGHTNIN' GRACE.

A LIGHT, A STAIN UPON THE LAND.

A RAPT'ROUS WRECK TO BLAME.

OH SAY, WHAT CAN THE HEAVENS SEE

BEYOND THIS FIERY DAY?

A CHILD AWAITS ETERNITY

A-WINKIN' AT THE GRAVE.

*Ali sleeps. Evelyn walks onto the porch, from within the house.*

EVELYN: She fall asleep?

LEXIE: Yeh.

EVELYN: Just like when she was…

LEXIE: Yeh.

*A moment.*

EVELYN: Should take her inside.

LEXIE: 'Fraid she'll wake.

EVELYN: As spent as she is?

LEXIE: All right.

*Lexie carries Ali in her arms.*

EVELYN: Think she's gonna be okay?

LEXIE: Just needs to rest.

EVELYN: Should take her to a doc anyway.

LEXIE: In the mornin'.

EVELYN: Have her checked out, make sure she don't got anythin' internal…

*Lexie carries Ali into the house, away from view. Evelyn sits on the porch, looking out. She sings to herself a slightly revised reprise of the song, lost in memory.*

### "Born to burn (reprise)"

EVELYN (CONT): ALL OF US ARE BORN TO BURN;

BORN ALONG THE WAY.

SUDDEN FLASH OF WEARY BIRDS

SHOW US LIGHTNIN' GRACE.

A LIGHT, A FLAME UPON THE LAND,

A LING'RIN PLACE TO NAME.

OH SAY, WHAT CAN THE SWALLOWS SEE

ALONG THE CINDERIN' SKY?

*Lexie walks in, and finishes the song with Evelyn. Note: Evelyn leads in the singing.*

LEXIE AND EVELYN: A CHILD AWAITS ETERNITY

FORGETTIN' SHE HAS CRIED.

*A moment.*

EVELYN: Such an awful song.

LEXIE: Ain't.

EVELYN: All death and flame and sadness. Every time I sing it...

LEXIE: Think of Momma?

EVELYN: It was her song.

*Brief moment.*

LEXIE: Should visit her.

EVELYN: Last I went, her headstone was cracked a bit.

LEXIE: Complain 'bout?

EVELYN: Like anybody gonna listen. Kids always in there drinkin' and messin' about. Why it is they wanna go have a party in a graveyard?

LEXIE: We used to do it.

EVELYN: I never.

LEXIE: Come on.

EVELYN: No.

LEXIE: Get a case of beer, bag of weed, go on out to the cemetery up on that little hill overlookin' the river... Stars look bright as flags hung up in the sky when you're out there. Like you're cheatin' death.

EVELYN: Still wrong.

LEXIE: Yes, ma'am.

EVELYN: Quit with that.

LEXIE *(with a smile)*: Yes, ma'am.

*A moment.*

EVELYN: Three hundred dollars.

LEXIE: Yeh.

EVELYN: Crazy.

LEXIE: Crazy she won.

EVELYN: Against some man too. Must've been drunk.

LEXIE: Don't rag her on about it in the mornin'.

EVELYN: Won't.

LEXIE: Know how you get.

EVELYN: …

LEXIE: Let her have this, okay? I mean, it was wrong her doin' what she did. But you gotta let her have this win. Needs it.

EVELYN: How long have I been dealin' with-?

LEXIE: I'm tellin' you.

EVELYN: All right.

*A moment.*

EVELYN (CONT): Gonna be mornin' soon.

LEXIE: You should get some sleep.

EVELYN: Not gonna. This whole day's been too…

*Lexie lights a cigarette.*

EVELYN (CONT): Eat at all?

LEXIE: *shakes head.*

EVELYN: Gotta eat.

LEXIE: Got protein bar in the room.

EVELYN: Protein bar is not food. How 'bout I get you somethin'

LEXIE: It's late.

EVELYN: There's some mac and cheese in the fridge.

LEXIE: Throw that out.

EVELYN: Still good.

LEXIE: Been there how long?

EVELYN: …

LEXIE: Know what I'd like?

EVELYN: …?

LEXIE: One of them crunchy casseroles Momma used to make.

EVELYN: Green bean.

LEXIE: Sometimes when I was over there, the taste of that casserole would just come to my mouth… Crunchy green bean casserole.

EVELYN: Could make it for you.

LEXIE: Got the recipe?

EVELYN: Momma gave it to me, 'fore she…

> *Brief moment.*

LEXIE: Sean in the same-?

EVELYN: No. They buried him on the other side of town. Where the rest of his kin are.

LEXIE: Visit him?

EVELYN: Went every week after the funeral, but… Just couldn't after a while.

LEXIE: Marry Hector.

EVELYN: Givin' me orders, private?

LEXIE: You're good for each other.

EVELYN: He's already married.

LEXIE: Left, didn't she?

EVELYN: Well…

LEXIE: Don't have to do church. Could do somethin' private. Just to acknowledge it between the two of you.

EVELYN: …Gotta get Ali and you sorted out first.

LEXIE: Take care of ourselves.

EVELYN: Ain't right.

LEXIE: Got some cross you wanna bear?

EVELYN: We're family.

LEXIE: Family don't mean you gotta sacrifice your whole life… Ain't been kids for a long time. And you're still actin' like you gotta have the whole world on your shoulders. That is no way to live. No, ma'am.

EVELYN: Wouldn't understand.

LEXIE: Where have I been?

EVELYN: Don't mean you know anythin' 'bout obligations...

LEXIE: ...That what we are?

EVELYN: Didn't mean...

LEXIE: You're not obliged to me in any way. Hell. If it weren't for you, I wouldn't have joined up in the first place. So, if we're gonna talk about who's obliged-

EVELYN: Never made you join up.

LEXIE: Okay.

EVELYN: When did I-?

LEXIE: Begged me.

EVELYN: Don't know what you're-

LEXIE: Sat out here and begged me. Christ. You forget all that?

EVELYN: I swear-

LEXIE: You sat out here in the dead of night, looked me in the eye and said I had to join up 'cuz those recruitment officers told us a good deal, and how else were we gonna get by? And if I didn't go, then it'd be Ali in five years time, and no way you were gonna let that happen, and I said I'd do it, for you, and for Dad, wherever the hell he is, and in Momma's memory, 'cuz that's what family does. Didn't say anythin' 'bout being obliged. And if it meant all of our lives might be just a little bit easier, 'cuz of some benefits down the line? All right.

EVELYN: Didn't have to…

LEXIE: Don't know what you been thinkin' all this time. And when they shipped me over there, I still didn't know what you were thinkin'. 'Cuz every time we emailed n shit, you wouldn't tell me nothin'. And I wouldn't tell you nothin'.

Even when… there was that day when… I wanted to scream out all kinds of shit to the only person who really knew me… I felt I couldn't tell you a goddamn thing. Even though the whole fuckin' thing was for…

EVELYN: Whatever I said…

LEXIE: Don't tell me you were drunk, 'cuz one thing I do know is that liquor and you don't get on. That's my domain. And Daddy's. Daddy was the liquor man 'round here. Though we don't say word. No, ma'am. We act like he's dead, when you know full well he ain't.

EVELYN: Don't know where he is.

LEXIE: Don't mean he's dead.

EVELYN: Ain't gonna start lookin' for Dad. It's been near twenty-

LEXIE: Eighteen.

EVELYN: And he never once wanted to reach out in all that time. So yeah, he's dead to me. The way he left us and Momma with Ali just born…

LEXIE: Went to fight.

EVELYN: And then he came back and what? Left again…for good.

LEXIE: Was sick.

EVELYN: Gonna tell me some story now?

LEXIE: Said he didn't feel well.

EVELYN: When he-?

LEXIE: 'fore he left… (*mimicking Evelyn*) for good.

EVELYN: Ain't told Momma that. Never told me that. Why the hell he tell you for?

LEXIE: *shrugs.*

EVELYN: Sick how?

LEXIE: Didn't say.

EVELYN: This some story-?

LEXIE: No, ma'am.

EVELYN: Well, you sure kept it quiet. Daddy sick from somethin' and he walks on out. And what, you been lookin' him up, seein' how he is?

LEXIE: Just thinkin'.

EVELYN: If you so much as tell me you are tryin' to make contact with him, I swear I will-

LEXIE: Throw me out?

EVELYN: Ain't said-

LEXIE: Don't you wanna see him?

EVELYN: No. I do not. If he was sick then, I'm sorry. I really am. But what he did was wrong and no, I will never forgive him.

LEXIE: …Sometimes I just wanna go back to that time when we were all…

EVELYN: …Listen… You've got to…

LEXIE: Find a job, forget about everythin', like everybody else?

EVELYN: What you been through…

LEXIE: Got no idea.

EVELYN: I can-

LEXIE: No. You can't. No fuckin' movie is gonna make you imagine how it is.

EVELYN: …You know, in church they say…

LEXIE: The road to Damascus is a long road?

EVELYN: …

LEXIE: Well, let me tell you, it is a bloody road. And I don't wish anybody on it, even if it does lead to Jesus.

EVELYN: … I did not make you join up.

LEXIE: We all put together our memories how we like.

EVELYN: You are NOT gonna put this on me. Won't let you.

LEXIE: Best throw me out, then. Put me in the same godforsaken place you put Daddy in mind.

*A moment.*

EVELYN: The day you were born, the day you were born, Momma put you in my arms, and said "This is your sister Alexandra Ray. Gotta take care of her from now on. Gotta be good to her." And every day, every single day since, that is ALL I've ever done. I don't know what you see when you look at me. Don't know what you imagine was said in this house. But everythin' I've ever done has been for you. And I don't say that all high n mighty. Say it with pride and love. And with the little words I got. … 'Cuz y'know, I could've gone off to college, after Momma passed. Could've let y'all stay in some foster home or get split up with strangers, but I didn't. I stayed. And Momma's sis, may she rest in peace, helped out too–

LEXIE: Why are you-?

EVELYN: 'Cuz you're still thinkin' about some long ago past that never was. And you keep at me and at me like I'm one of them punchin' bags Ali likes to knock about. … This here is all you got. Ain't nothin' else.

LEXIE: …

EVELYN: Now, it is late. And I got Ali in there all bruised to hell, and I gotta get more alterations done, and bake some muffins, so I can get them to the coffee shop in the mornin' to see if they sell… so… You wanna sit out here, smoke, think on… whatever…? Go on.

*Evelyn goes inside the house.*

*A moment.*

### "Cadence without a name"

LEXIE *(IMPROVISING A CADENCE)*: I KNOW ME AND I KNOW YOU.

THREE CHEERS FOR [THE] RED, WHITE AND BLUE.

FUNNY HOW AS TIME GOES ON, ALL OUR DAYS ARE SAID AND DONE.

YOU GO THIS WAY, I GO THAT.

'NOTHER DEATH IN SECONDS FLAT.

*Lexie walks into the field, and out of sight.*

## Scene Six

*EXT. The following morning. On the porch. Ali slowly walks out, barefoot. She clearly is feeling the hurt all through her body this morning, and much less the sense of exhilaration she felt last night. She looks out. It is hot, humid and sticky.*

*She is about to head back inside when she stumbles across a cigarette butt, left behind. She picks it up, puts it to her nose, smells it. A sense of recognition. She places it between her fingers and pretends to smoke it, mimicking Lexie.*

*Evelyn calls to Ali from inside the house, as if she were in another room.*

EVELYN *(from Off)*: Gotta get some breakfast in you. Get on up, Ali.

*Ali pockets the cigarette butt.*

ALI *(softly)*: Here.

EVELYN *(from Off)*: …You hear me?

ALI *(calling out)*: Here, Evelyn.

*EVELYN walks out, from within.*

EVELYN: What you doin' out? It's hot.

ALI: Like it.

EVELYN: …Look a sight.

ALI: Road warrior.

EVELYN: Road warrior, my ass. Pretty girl like you…

*Evelyn gives her a small kiss on the forehead.*

ALI: Ow.

EVELYN: Crazy girl.

ALI: Think I scared them all last night when they saw how dope I was. Should've seen them. Had this stunned look in their eyes.

EVELYN: Stunned?

ALI: Like, partin' the waters stunned.

EVELYN: Okay, Miss Featherweight-

ALI: Flyweight.

EVELYN: Flyweight Champion of the World, you're gonna have breakfast or what?

ALI: *thinks a while.*

EVELYN *(heads back inside)*: Well, while you make up your mind, I'm gonna-

ALI: Hotcakes.

EVELYN: That all-?

ALI: Pigs-in-a-blanket hotcakes.

EVELYN: Want to make me work, huh?

ALI: Haven't had in a long time.

EVELYN: I'll throw some bacon on-

ALI: Hot dogs!

EVELYN: Huh?

ALI: Can't do pigs-in-a-blanket with bacon. Gotta be hot dogs. And then you roll the hotcake round the hot dog and-

EVELYN: All right, Top Chef.

*Evelyn goes back inside.*

*A bird perches on a nearby tree. Ali looks at it. Perhaps she hums a little improvised tune as she looks at it.*

*Hector walks in, from the field. He has a gift-wrapped box in hand. He looks at Ali looking at the bird.*

HECTOR: That bird callin' to you?

ALI: Just givin' me a smile.

HECTOR: Some bird, eh?

ALI: Wants its freedom.

*After slight moment, the bird flies away.*

HECTOR: Got it now, looks like.

ALI: Yeah.

HECTOR: … Here.

*Hector tosses her the gift-wrapped box.*

ALI: What's this?

HECTOR: Open it.

ALI: Not my birthday or-

HECTOR: Christ All Mighty, you Glimmer Girls are all alike. Just open it, Ali. Ain't gonna bring you any harm.

*Ali tears through gift-wrap and opens the box.*

ALI: Where'd you-?

HECTOR: Think I've never done anythin' in my life? Won the region when I was in junior high. 'Fore my heart thing kicked in.

*Ali reveals a small boxing trophy.*

ALI: Beautiful.

HECTOR: It's for you.

ALI: …?

HECTOR: Won last night, right?

ALI: …How many you beat?

HECTOR: Region? Bunch of kids. There was this one kid, though. Real sonofabitch.

ALI: Yeah?

HECTOR: Super-mean. And for no reason, too. Had it in his head he was gonna do me in before he knocked me out.

ALI: What'd you do?

HECTOR: I suffered for a while.

ALI: Why?

HECTOR: Fake him out. Then, just when he thought he had me, I lay into him – left, right, uppercut, jab, jab, punch, punch... He was so tired he couldn't come back at me.

ALI: Strategy.

HECTOR: It's all in the mind.

ALI: How come you never told me 'bout-?

HECTOR: Man ain't nothin' if he don't got secrets.

ALI *(lightly)*: Bull.

EVELYN *(from off)*: Don't you pester her, sugar man.

HECTOR: Nothin' of the kind, Evelyn Jane.

*Evelyn walks in with plate of hot dogs wrapped in hotcakes.*

EVELYN *(to Ali)*: Here you go, baby doll.

HECTOR: Helluva lot of pigs-in-a-blanket.

EVELYN: Not for you.

*Ali eats.*

EVELYN (CONT): How they taste?

ALI: Good.

HECTOR: I'd like some too, if-

EVELYN: Go ahead.

*He eats.*

EVELYN (CONT, to Hector): Slow down, honey. Not catchin' a train or anythin'.

HECTOR *(food in mouth)*: Eatin'.

EVELYN: Not chewin'. *(to Ali)* Is he chewin'?

ALI: Not much.

HECTOR: All right. Chewin'.

EVELYN: What's that there?

ALI: Huh?

EVELYN: Not blind, Ali. What is that?

ALI: Trophy. Hector gave.

HECTOR: Just a present.

EVELYN: It is one thing to try to win me over, but there is no need for you to try to win my sister over too.

HECTOR: Ain't tryin'-

ALI: He won it in junior high.

EVELYN: That right?

HECTOR: Had a little talent for the boxin' thing.

EVELYN: Don't remember that.

HECTOR: Weren't interested in me, then.

EVELYN *(joking)*: Who says I'm interested now?

HECTOR: … Lexie not comin' down?

EVELYN: …?

HECTOR: Breakfast.

EVELYN: Gone.

ALI: Gone where?

EVELYN: Don't know.

HECTOR: What the hell you-?

EVELYN: I gotta get a move on this mornin' or -

ALI: Where'd she go, Evelyn?

EVELYN: She can go wherever the hell she wants. It's not like we gotta be after her all the time.

HECTOR: Fight again?

EVELYN: We do not fight.

ALI (*as a challenge*): Huh.

EVELYN: Got enough shit goin' on, don't need-

HECTOR: No good you two fightin'.

EVELYN: I'm aware, Hector. Well aware.

ALI: Want me to see if she's-?

EVELYN: You are sittin' yourself down, finishin' your breakfast, and then we are goin' to urgent care, get you checked out.

ALI: Don't need…

EVELYN: Make sure everythin's-

ALI: Why you gotta push Lexie out all the time? She's a hero, and you're bitchin' at her all the goddamn fuckin' time.

EVELYN: What are you-?

ALI: She come back, right? After all the mess she's been through over there… And you gotta…

EVELYN: I did not-

ALI: Fuckin' messed up to shit.

EVELYN: Ali.

ALI: You can screw yourselves, screw yourselves if you think I'm goin' to some fuckin' doc or do anythin' 'round here!

*Ali grabs trophy and goes into the house.*

EVELYN: Ali?

*SFX: We hear perhaps door slam from her bedroom.*

HECTOR: …If you keep on fightin'…

EVELYN: We are not-

HECTOR: Why Ali run off, get herself into a fight last night? EVELYN: …

HECTOR: Why Lexie run off?

EVELYN: Hasn't…

HECTOR: Not here, is she?

EVELYN: … Don't know what business it is of yours-

HECTOR: If we are gonna live together…

EVELYN: Hector…

HECTOR: If we are gonna live together, then what happens here is my business. It's not just about helpin' you out with the mortgage and-

EVELYN: I never asked to-

HECTOR: And you don't need to ask. 'Cuz I will help you out. 'Cuz that's what people do for each other when they're together. But I won't stand… Can't stand to see you havin' it out with your sisters all the goddamn time.

EVELYN: Not all-

HECTOR: Ever since Lexie get back, you've been nothin' but clawin' and scratchin' every which way.

EVELYN: That is not-

HECTOR: Listen, I love you, but I can't watch a family tearin' at each other like this. Grew up like this. … I look at you, and I see the world. World so big and full of hunger and silence and ache, it'll just about break from all the cursin' it's doin' inside. And I think "What kind of fiery song kicks at her dreams? What kind of rage is it that gets hold of her, so she doesn't even think 'bout what she's sayin' half the time? And why do her eyes burn and close over like a storm when anyone ever tries to come close?"

EVELYN: …

HECTOR: Got rules for everythin', Evelyn. But sometimes, you gotta let up on them rules, so people can live their lives. … Lexie goin' through stuff? Hell yeah. … God knows she'll be goin' through stuff for a long, long time. But you can't make her into somethin' she's not. And can't make Ali either. But what you can make is family.

EVELYN: ... Peace, forgiveness and whole lotta understandin'?

HECTOR: Want a life, baby. Real life, and not some hell-bent mess of a thing.

EVELYN: Find someone else, then.

HECTOR: Do not...

EVELYN: ...

HECTOR: I am right here, baby. Right here. Understand?

*A moment.*

EVELYN: Don't know if I...

HECTOR *(casting the dream)*: We'll make it up, Evelyn. We'll make our whole lives up. Like them birds up there chasin' their freedom. We'll roam 'bout, even if it's only in our minds, and see what's cookin' up there in that sky.

EVELYN *(softly)*: ... All right.

HECTOR: What's that?

EVELYN: All right.

HECTOR: Glory be!

*He takes her in his arms, kisses her.*

EVELYN: Don't get all crazy now.

HECTOR: I'm gonna get you that cake you want.

EVELYN: We'll talk 'bout.

HECTOR: I'll do right by you, Evelyn. You won't need for anythin'.

EVELYN: Don't be layin' it on thick! You are this close to-

HECTOR: Now, I'll take Ali to the...

EVELYN: But you-

HECTOR: Got Walker coverin' for me at the dealership today. Rest. [you] Need it, Glimmer Girl.

EVELYN: Gonna have to stop callin' me that. The name's-

HECTOR (*calls out*): Ali, how 'bout we go to urgent care, get you checked out? ... (*to Evelyn*) And when Lexie gets back, get her a soda or sweet tea or somethin', and just... y'know?

EVELYN: You're a stubborn man, Hector Johnson.

HECTOR: (*calls out*) Ali!

*After brief moment, Ali appears.*

ALI: If there's some kinda line at urgent care, I'm not waitin'.

HECTOR: Okay.

ALI (*to Evelyn*): And I am not makin' up. Just... still hurt, so...

EVELYN: Gotta get a comb through that hair of yours.

HECTOR: She's fine, Evelyn. We got it sorted out.

ALI: Call us when Lexie-?

EVELYN: I will.

ALI: Mean it.

*Hector and Ali head out. As they do so:*

HECTOR: You know, you can get a trophy like the one I got, too.

ALI: Yeah?

HECTOR: Get into a real match, in proper league. Absolutely.

*They are gone from view. Evelyn remains. She prays: a call to the gods.*

EVELYN: Oh light, oh light of mine, Shine heaven upon us.

## Scene Seven

*EXT. Night. On the hill overlooking the river at the town cemetery. Lexie is drinking beer. It is clear she has been drinking for a while. She shout-sings a mash-up of two army cadences. A ritual, a release, a blues...*

### "Captain Jack/Momma, Momma"

LEXIE: HEY, HEY CAPTAIN JACK
MEET ME DOWN BY THE RAILROAD SHACK,
WITH THAT BOTTLE IN YOUR HAND,
I'M GONNA BE A DRINKIN' MAN,

MOMMA, MOMMA DONCHA CRY,
YOUR LITTLE GIRL AIN'T GONNA DIE.
MOMMA, MOMMA DONCHA CRY,
YOUR LITTLE GIRL'S NOT GONNA DIE.

HEY, HEY CAPTAIN JACK
MEET ME DOWN BY THE RAILROAD SHACK,
WITH THAT RIFLE IN YOUR HAND

*VAUGHN appears. He continues the cadence.*

VAUGHN: I'M GONNA BE A SHOOTIN' MAN,

MOMMA, MOMMA DON'T YOU SEE
WHAT THE ARMY'S DONE TO ME?
MOMMA, MOMMA CAN'T YOU SEE
WHAT THE ARMY'S...

*Brief moment.*

VAUGHN (CONT): Just get back?

LEXIE: Yeah.

VAUGHN: Man, I had me those calls in mind for months after I got back. Never change, huh?

LEXIE: No, sir.

VAUGHN: Name's Vaughn. You?

LEXIE: Lexie.

VAUGHN: Got a beer, Lexie?

*She hands him beer. He takes it, opens can, drinks.*

VAUGHN (CONT): Nice out here, huh?

LEXIE: My momma's buried here.

VAUGHN: Nicest cemetery in these here parts. Most others don't got a view of the river. They keep the grounds nice, too.

LEXIE: When'd you serve, Vaughn?

VAUGHN: 'Nother century.

LEXIE: That long ago?

VAUGHN: I'm what they call "prehistoric."

LEXIE: Don't look it.

VAUGHN: Feel it. My bones are a creakin' mess. ...
Lookin' to finish off all that beer?

LEXIE: Workin' on it.

VAUGHN: If you wanna get drunk, there's a bar down
cemetery lane.

LEXIE: I know.

VAUGHN: Familiar, then?

LEXIE: This is home.

VAUGHN: Just you?

LEXIE: Huh?

VAUGHN: No other family?

LEXIE: Sisters.

VAUGHN: They serve too?

LEXIE: No.

VAUGHN: So, it's just you.

LEXIE: Not like that.

VAUGHN: Don't see your sisters out here with you.

LEXIE: They got stuff.

VAUGHN: And your stuff's not their stuff. Am I right?

LEXIE: ...

VAUGHN: Had family once. Know how these things go.

LEXIE: Wanted to be near Momma. That's all.

VAUGHN: Where she at?

LEXIE: Headstone's over there.

VAUGHN: Where that mess of wildflowers-?

LEXIE: Yeah.

VAUGHN: … Tell her you're back?

LEXIE: Uh-huh.

VAUGHN: But you didn't give her the full run-down, did you?

LEXIE: Don't need.

VAUGHN: Never give the full run-down. 'Cuz it just freaks people out. *(reaches for beer)* Mind if I-?

LEXIE: Go ahead.

VAUGHN: Thanks, soldier.

*A moment as they both drink.*

VAUGHN *(CONT, recalls cadence)*: HEY, HEY CAPTAIN JACK.

MEET ME DOWN BY THE SHITTY SHACK.

LEXIE *(laughing)*: Not how it goes.

VAUGHN: That's how we ended up sayin' it back in BT. Y'all never made anythin' up?

LEXIE: Well…

VAUGHN: Gotta make things up.

LEXIE: Sometimes.

VAUGHN: … Your Momma know you went over?

LEXIE: No. She… passed when I was a little girl.

VAUGHN: Sorry.

LEXIE: Don't think she would've ever expected me to join up, let alone go over. Had enough with my Dad.

VAUGHN: He served?

LEXIE: Army Strong. Yes, sir.

VAUGHN: Thought you said you only had sisters left. He buried here too?

LEXIE: No.

VAUGHN: Went AWOL on you?

LEXIE: …

VAUGHN: Helluva mess, ain't it?

LEXIE: Yes, sir.

> *She grabs another beer, opens can, drinks.*

VAUGHN: Take it easy there, soldier.

LEXIE: Hell with it.

> *She keeps drinking.*

LEXIE *(CONT, reveling, song-like)*: Ol' Carolina moon, shine on me.

VAUGHN *(echoing, in kind)*: Ol' Carolina moon, shine your light.

LEXIE: Goddamn Carolina moon.

*Brief moment.*

VAUGHN: Bar much better place to get drunk than out here.

LEXIE: Like it out here.

VAUGHN: Dead bodies, worms, maggots, bones, flowers, blossoms, trees, stones.

LEXIE: Yeah.

VAUGHN *(part of a cadence)*: Fall in, maggot.

LEXIE *(perhaps enacting salute etc.)*: Yes, sir. Whatever you say, sir.

VAUGHN: Girl, you are drunker than I am.

LEXIE: Hold my liquor good. Learned from the best.

VAUGHN: Sergeant Major?

LEXIE: My Daddy taught me.

VAUGHN: He a drinkin' man?

LEXIE: Part of a long line. Moonshine and tobacco.

VAUGHN: Rotten country.

LEXIE: What we're made.

VAUGHN: ...Where you think he gone to?

LEXIE: Don't know. Not like he ever sent postcards.

VAUGHN *(quoting postcard tag line)*: Wish you were here.

LEXIE: Fuck that.

*She finishes beer. Smashes beer can with boot.*

LEXIE (CONT): Sometimes I think he's up in Alberta or somethin'.

VAUGHN: Canada?

LEXIE: Picture him there, sittin' along the tar sands.

VAUGHN: What's that?

LEXIE: What they got up there.

VAUGHN: Sands made of tar?

LEXIE: Crude oil. Mines. Little patch of skinny trees where forest used to be.

VAUGHN: Why'd you picture him there?

LEXIE: 'Cuz Daddy used to talk about it when he was still 'round. Said some of his kin, way, way back, were from up there. Back when they had rolling fen and people would fish their walleye straight from the stream. Always thought he'd be happy there somehow, even if he was only sittin' in dirty sand. 'Least he'd be with some of his people.

VAUGHN: Think 'bout goin'?

LEXIE: It's far.

VAUGHN: Maybe you'd see him.

LEXIE: Wouldn't recognize me anymore. I was a little girl last we seen each other.

VAUGHN: Not soldier?

LEXIE: Hell no. He would've had a laugh 'bout that. *(mimicking her father)* "My little girl a soldier? That's some kind of moon talk." No. Back then I wanted to be a baton twirler.

VAUGHN: Not a job.

LEXIE: Teacher would say, "Alexandra Ray Glimord, what do you want to be when you grow up?" And I'd be, like, "One of them girls with batons."

*Vaughn sings a song from memory.*

### "Twirlin' Girl"

VAUGHN: TWIRLIN' GIRL, TWIRLIN' GIRL,

WHAT WILL YOU SPIN FOR ME?

TWIRLIN' GIRL, ALIGHT THE WORLD

MUCH FURTHER THAN THE SEA.

HEY NOW, TWIRLIN' GIRL.

SING A SONG FOR ME.

ABOUT THE WAY THE LIGHTNIN' WHIRL

QUICKENS GOD'S MERCY.

*Brief moment.*

LEXIE: What's that?

VAUGHN: Song I heard once.

LEXIE: Sounds like one of Momma's songs.

VAUGHN: She a singer?

LEXIE: Just for us. She'd make little songs up.

VAUGHN: Don't know where I heard it.

LEXIE: It's nice.

VAUGHN *(half-sings)*: Twirlin' girl, twirlin' girl… *(and then, says)* Always wanted me a little girl.

LEXIE: Yeh?

VAUGHN: To tell stories to, tuck into bed at night.

LEXIE: …Got someone here?

VAUGHN: This ground?

LEXIE: *shakes head.*

VAUGHN: Got kin everywhere.

LEXIE: Yeah?

VAUGHN: Name a place.

LEXIE: You're shittin' me.

VAUGHN: Name one.

LEXIE: Okay. Uh. Charleston?

VAUGHN: Yeah.

LEXIE: Sharpsburg?[3]

VAUGHN: Yeah.

LEXIE: …Okinawa?

VAUGHN: Crossin' continents now?

LEXIE: Said everywhere.

VAUGHN: Yeah.

LEXIE: Inchon?

VAUGHN: Yeah.

LEXIE: Saigon?

VAUGHN: Yeah.

LEXIE: … Kuwait?

VAUGHN: Uh-huh.

LEXIE: Basra?

VAUGHN: Yeah.

LEXIE: Kandahar?

VAUGHN: Yeah.

LEXIE: Kabul?

VAUGHN: Yeah.

---

[3] Once called Antietam in Virginia.

LEXIE: … Montgomery?

VAUGHN: …Whole mess in Montgomery.

LEXIE: [that's a] Lotta kin.

VAUGHN: Walkin' the earth in tired rags and smelly feet, stinkin' it up with the mess of death and existence.

LEXIE: Don't see how you can get 'round to them all.

VAUGHN: It's easier with them that are close. Not that I mourn any of the others any less. That's the strange thing 'bout mournin': ain't somethin' you can buy or sell. It just is. 'Course, 'round here? All sorts of kin-ship twisted 'round here.

LEXIE: How you figure?

VAUGHN: Well, see that barn swallow up there perched on that stump of a tree?

LEXIE: Uh-huh.

VAUGHN: Barn swallow got no business there.

LEXIE: Can do what he like.

VAUGHN: No. Supposed to be further south by this time. But it sits there doin' its flappity-flap, and we say "all right," 'cuz it's scared, like we're scared. Scared of what's 'round us, inside us, what's way over yonder.

LEXIE: Ain't.

VAUGHN: Fear's so deep inside, we don't even know it's there…. Get up in the mornin' complain 'bout the day. Go to bed at night, worried sick 'bout gettin' sick. Walk about with a mess of wars in our head and nowhere to put them. No-the-fuck-where.

So, what we do? We toss 'em into the trash, try to forget... Why, we even stop callin' them wars, 'cuz we can't bring ourselves to call them that anymore. 'Cuz what it make us think of? Dead babies. Piles and piles of poor dead babies don't even know what hit 'em. And it's a sadness we can't bear. 'Cuz we put it there. No one else. We put it into the world. And ain't no sands of tar gonna make them go away.

So, we come here, look out onto the dirty river, and think about whether we should fix on goin' in, and end it all with a mighty splash, or stay out here and get ourselves piss drunk so we can keep on forgettin'.

'Cept the thing is, it don't go away. No, ma'am. The forgettin' has a way of comin' on back and gettin' in your face when you least expect. Like, you can be sittin' out here prayin' over somebody's grave, and all of a sudden, all the stuff you pushed down and away into that forgettin' place just stares at you with the full weight of its presence. And you can't move, speak, or see for nothin'. Why, you can't even taste. Food is like

VAUGHN (CONT): sandpaper on your tongue. And that's when you think: what we need is a kinda reckonin' to shed a little light.

LEXIE (*as if some other where, half to herself, the night wears on*): Ol' Carolina moon, shine your light...

*As he speaks, a kind of spell begins to take hold.*

VAUGHN: So, you start prayin' to the gods you never prayed to before -'cuz you thought you were done with prayer - all that was some other life – but it turns out, you need it. So, you get down on your knees, bow your head and ask the gods for whatever they can give you to bring you back to yourself again.

LEXIE: And what do the gods say?

VAUGHN: The gods don't say anythin'. 'Cuz they wanna make you work for it.

LEXIE: Drill Sergeant gods.

VAUGHN: That's right. So, you pray again. A little harder. You push your knees into the earth until they are bleedin' from comin' up 'gainst the rock. And you hope with everythin' in your heart that this time, this time, the gods will answer your callin'.

LEXIE: And?

VAUGHN: Well, these being tough, stubborn gods who know way too much about you and all you've done and what you've gone through, they take their time. They wanna test you. While all the while your knees are battered to shit, your mouth is dry and your ears can't hear anythin' 'cept a high constant sound, like the sound an M16 makes after it has fired a couple dozen rounds.

LEXIE: Know that.

VAUGHN: Yeah?

LEXIE: Yes, sir.

VAUGHN: So, this is when the gods make a decision.

LEXIE: Yeah?

VAUGHN: They may be tough gods, but they're not un-necessarily cruel. After all, they can see into your heart. And if you've a good heart…

LEXIE: Yeah.

VAUGHN: They cut you a deal.

LEXIE: What kind?

VAUGHN: Poker or blackjack kind.

LEXIE: Nah.

VAUGHN: Think I'm lyin', soldier? Think WHERE the fuck-all I've been makes me some kind of sonofabitch two-bit liar?

LEXIE: No.

VAUGHN: The gods say: If you carry on with your mess of a life on this here messy earth made of fire and chaos, and you live it right and honor those that are good to you and do right by you, be they family or friends or whatnot, then maybe, maybe we'll give you a chance to move, speak, see, hear, and taste again. Just like you done when you were a child and it felt like everythin' was possible in this here world.

LEXIE: Would like that.

VAUGHN: So, you get up off your bloody knees and you look out onto the river again and you give it a kind of smile – like the VAUGHN (CONT): kind of smile that says "Later, mister. Someday later we'll meet each other in the flesh." – and you try to remember where the hell you are. 'Cuz by this time the ground feels like every ground you've ever walked upon, from here to the far reaches of the burnin' desert and back.

So, you start to listen to the murmur of the trees and the drops of rain that fall upon the leaves, and start to smell tobacco. Everywhere. And this time, the smell don't put you out, don't make you feel like a goddamn maggot or somethin', but makes you feel like home.

And that's when you take a step, and walk on back to where you've been, and where people that love you are waitin' for you, been waitin', for a long time.

LEXIE: And as you walk, you hear a little song that you remember your Daddy sung to you once, when he was clear-eyed and un-beset by trouble. And you think: how is it that I am hearin' this song again when there's no way in the world...?

VAUGHN: Hear it 'cuz it's inside you.

LEXIE: ...And it sings:

### "Troubled Child"

LEXIE (CONT): GO ON, GO ON, MY TROUBLED CHILD

VAUGHN: LET ALL YOUR RAGE SUBSIDE.

SEND 'LONG YOUR BLOODY SACRIFICE

LEXIE: BEYOND THE RIVER WIDE.

VAUGHN: GO ON, DEAR CHILD OF MINE.

*Vaughn kisses Lexie on the forehead.*

*A moment.*

*Lexie walks away.*

*Vaughn looks at her.*

*Mid-journey, she turns back,*

*But Vaughn has disappeared.*

## Scene Eight

*EXT. Evening. On the porch. Evelyn is sitting on the porch. Ali is standing.*

ALI: Can't sit out here all night.

EVELYN: Wait as long as I have to.

ALI: But you've been-

EVELYN: KNOW what I'm doin'.

ALI: … If you hadn't pissed each other off…

EVELYN: If you are goin' to get on that again, best go to sleep, leave me out here in peace.

ALI: … No peace.

EVELYN: What you say?

ALI: No peace to be had.

EVELYN: That somethin' Hector said when you went to the doc?

ALI: No.

EVELYN: Came up with that all by yourself?

ALI: Think I don't think things?

EVELYN: Oh, I know you think. That's why I keep tellin' you, you should do more than…

ALI: I will.

EVELYN: …Yeah?

ALI: See maybe if some classes open up at that college.

EVELYN: You know, they got a good sports ed program. Could make a livin' with that. Schools will cut everythin' else come budget time, but they will leave sports.

ALI: We'll see. … [you] Really gonna marry Hector?

EVELYN: That what he tell you?

ALI: Couldn't stop beamin' about it. All the way in the car.

EVELYN: Gonna give it a little try. Not formal weddin', of course, but…

ALI: Do a party?

EVELYN: Can't even think about that right now.

ALI: Be nice to have a party.

EVELYN: Celebrate?

ALI: Somethin'.

EVELYN: … Sometimes I think there's nothin' worth celebratin' anymore. All's just…

ALI (*lightly*): Crap.

EVELYN: … Don't know what it all means, bein' here, goin' on.

ALI: What you talkin'?

EVELYN: Get up in the mornin', don't know what to do about anythin'…

ALI: Fix the roof.

EVELYN: Huh?

ALI: Got three hundred dollars, right?

EVELYN: Think that's all it's goin' to take?

ALI: It's a start.

EVELYN: …Lexie would say, when you were little… she'd say we were a big ol' mess, and it didn't matter if the house and everythin' else was a mess, too, 'cuz if we put it all together, somehow we'd make somethin' whole.

ALI: … Like somethin' Momma would say.

EVELYN: Strange, right?

ALI: 'Cuz Lexie and Momma…

EVELYN: Not a bit alike.

*A moment.*

ALI: Think she'll…?

EVELYN: Pray she'll…

ALI: Been gone so long…

EVELYN: When I think about Lexie wanderin' the earth like that with all the stuff she's got inside…

ALI: … What if she don't come back? What if she keeps on wanderin' and wanderin' 'til she don't even remember we're here at all, and just loses herself in the goddamn fuckin' burnin' shit of the earth?

EVELYN: Can't think…

ALI: Daddy done.

EVELYN: That was different.

ALI: How is that different? How the fuck is that different?

EVELYN: …

ALI: Not even Barry knows where the hell she is.

EVELYN: That Barry can kiss my ass with his doomsday shit.

ALI: Ain't dooms-

EVELYN: If he's sayin' anythin' 'bout Lexie never comin' back… I don't wanna hear it.

ALI: But-

EVELYN: No!

*A moment.*

*SFX: Phone rings, inside the house.*

ALI: I'll get it.

*Ali bolts into the house, picks up ringing phone. The phone conversation cannot be heard from outside.*

*Evelyn sings fervently to herself – a summoning. One of her hands is clenched into a fist. She pounds fist into the palm of her other hand. A ritual as she sings, a call to some other heaven.*

**"Blessed are the few"**

EVELYN: LIGHT, OH LIGHT, OH LIGHT OF MINE.

BLESSED ARE THE FEW.

WHO ROAM THE EARTH FOR WHAT IT'S WORTH

CRAP NICKEL, DIME OR TWO.

*She waits. Nothing.*

*She sings again with fist into palm.*

LIGHT, OH LIGHT, OH LIGHT OF MINE

BLESSED ARE THE...

WHO ROAM THE EARTH FOR WHAT ITS...

*Evelyn tries to continue the song, but finds that she cannot. She keeps on, fist into palm, fist into palm, fist into...*

*And then...*

*Lexie appears.*

LEXIE: Hey.

EVELYN: Lexie. Lexie. Where you been, crazy girl?

*Evelyn embraces Lexie fiercely.*

*Ali walks out, sees her two sisters in an embrace. She is quiet.*

*After a moment, Evelyn lets go gently.*

EVELYN (CONT): You all right?

LEXIE: ...

ALI *(drawing closer)*: Huh?

LEXIE: ...Hungry.

*Lights fade.*

*<u>End of Play.</u>*